Focus on the case, Matthews. This was not an accident, and you need to figure out how it's related, Owen told himself.

Miriam inhaled sharply. Her head shook back and forth, her face a mash of different emotions. Shock, denial, disbelief paraded across it. She obviously had read his lips accurately. She jumped to her feet; her words sped so fast her hands tripped over each other. "Someone stole my car? This is crazy! I have never done anything to the people in this town. Why do they want to hurt me like this?"

Owen backed a step away, reaching for his cell phone to put his mind on a different, more innocuous, track. "I'll call Wes to report the stolen car," he announced. "How far could it go on this island anyway? I'm sure we'll find it."

At the same time Owen would find out who was behind the threats and put a stop to them. Because there was only one thing worse than being responsible for destroying a pure heart.

Not protecting one.

KATY LEE

is an inspirational romantic-suspense author writing higher-purpose stories in high-speed worlds. She dedicates her life to sharing tales of love, from the greatest love story ever told to those sweet romantic stories of falling in love. She is the children's ministry director for her church as well as a leader of a Christian women's organization. Katy and her husband are both born New Englanders, but have been known to travel at the drop of a hat. As her homeschooled kids say, they consider themselves "world-schooled." But no matter where Katy is you can always find her at www.KatyLeeBooks.com anytime. She would love to connect with you.

WARNING SIGNS

KATY LEE

HARLEQUIN® LOVE INSPIRED® SUSPENSE

Recycling programs
for this product may
not exist in your area.

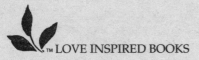

™ LOVE INSPIRED BOOKS

ISBN-13: 978-0-373-67580-7

WARNING SIGNS

www.Harlequin.com

Printed in U.S.A.

My sheep hear My voice,
and I know them, and they follow Me.
—*John* 10:27

Do not fear, for I am with you;
do not be dismayed, for I am your God.
I will strengthen you and help you;
I will uphold you with my righteous right hand.
—*Isaiah* 41:10

To the lovely ladies Sue and Val, who are our interpreters for our deaf brothers and sisters in Christ at my church. Your dedication to interpret every service allows many to "hear" the Lord's message. God bless you and your ministry.

ONE

Drug Enforcement agent Owen Matthews gripped the wheel of his rented sports boat as he coasted through the North Atlantic at barely half throttle. The Maine island town of Stepping Stones urged Owen to rush forward to the safety of its shores, but his newly acquired phobia of boats wouldn't let him speed up even one knot. At this rate the sun would be gone before he arrived at his next assignment.

"What we do for friends," Owen mumbled through clenched teeth, thinking about his old academy roommate, and the island's sheriff, Wesley Grant. Even though Wes had chosen small-town law enforcement and Owen had taken the federal route with the DEA down to the Mexican border, the two kept in touch.

Wes had called, needing Owen's undercover expertise to take down a recent marijuana problem at Stepping Stones High School. No job was too dangerous or too far for Owen when it came to extinguishing the distribution of illegal mind-altering substances. Even if the job brought him back to these Maine waters, where his guilt ran deep and he'd vowed never to go again.

Owen inhaled the old and familiar salty air…and cringed. He needed to get off this boat. He needed to get this job done and get back to Texas where he belonged.

He steered his focus to the few facts Wes had given him about the case, specifically on how the drugs had appeared about six months ago, soon after two new residents had moved to Stepping Stones.

Wes was a good cop, but he probably didn't want to believe a fellow islander could ever bring such harm down on one of his own. Since Owen grew up on the mainland and not with these people, he could offer a more unbiased investigation of all the inhabitants, new and old.

Plus, Owen knew firsthand how the ones closest to us had the power to destroy us. And he knew this not because he'd been on the receiving end, but because of the people he'd destroyed. His past offenses convinced him that anyone could be a suspect— including the owner of the fishing boat coming at him.

At first, the vessel bobbed alongside a huge rock and lighthouse up ahead. When it shot off like a bullet, Owen questioned its hurry. Was its retreat an innocent maneuver, or had Owen intruded on an illegal happening of some kind?

He kept his undercover status in mind and prepared to make all neighborly with the captain of the… He strained to read the name of the fishing boat scrawled on its hull.

The *Rita Ann.*

A harmless enough name. Although typically a drug trafficker wouldn't be advertising its wares on its exterior for the world to see. Owen observed more of the rusty, white fishing boat with its tall, lit masthead. A rule follower, it would seem, with his adequate safety equipment. But if one were carrying illegal cargo, it would be in his best interest to keep the lightbulbs in working order. Why risk the chance of being pulled over?

Owen searched the tinted pilothouse windows for the captain, but only the reflection of the setting sun glinted back at him. He closed in, waving his hand high, then slowed to an idle to wait for a response.

Instead, the *Rita Ann* increased its speed and changed its course—directly at him.

Stunned, Owen felt his hand slip off the gearshift. This couldn't be happening. Not again. The sun was setting, but he could still be seen. The last time it had been pitch-dark. This didn't make sense.

Snap out of it, Matthews! He ordered himself to reengage, but his stiff hands might as well have been petrified wood. He had to move, but past visions of a splintering boat flying sky-high immobilized his reflexes. Six years of time dissolved into this moment as he relived his first crash.

No. He wouldn't let history repeat itself. *Move! Now!*

A surge of adrenaline pushed him to hit Reverse. He blasted back out of the *Rita Ann*'s path. The fishing boat jetted past him without an acknowledgment.

Owen questioned whether the driver had seen him or not. How could he not, though? He watched the *Rita Ann* chug out to sea. Owen forced his hand to turn the wheel to follow. He would flag it down to find out, but first he would need to speed up to catch it.

Duty called, and Owen's previous driving-with-caution vaulted to the wind. He kicked up his speed a notch, then another and another. The front bow parted the rolling waves into a frothy wake as he set his sights on the *Rita Ann*.

With his attention drilled straight ahead, he nearly missed a gray object flying past him on his starboard side. Immediately another followed. Owen's head whipped from side to side while his mind registered what they were.

He slowed a bit to identify them as flat rocks, smaller, less visible than the large one with the lighthouse on it. Some even submerged. The sight of the solid, unmovable masses caused him to slam back the throttle, jolting the craft to a rumbling crawl.

The *Rita Ann* raced on ahead without him.

It wasn't the fact that he let her go that choked him, but rather that he could have had a disastrous collision if he had been a few scant feet more to his left.

At least no one was in the boat with me this time. Owen blew out a breath of anger at his stupidity. *I have no business being out on these waters. Not even for a job.*

With tighter fists than before, he gripped the steering wheel again. In an anxious cold sweat, Owen drifted with the tiniest bit of gas sent to the engine. In such a slow motion, he realized more and more of the rocks protruded up from the ocean floor around him, leading up to the island of Stepping Stones.

The island apparently got its name from these rocks. The lighthouse was built on the largest of them, while the others dotted a sporadic path. A beautiful scene for a painting, but in reality the rocks posed a deadly threat to boats cruising their way up the coast of New England. How the ferry could dock here was beyond him. Maybe that's why it only came in once a week. Too risky with these formidable pieces of stone that required a wide berth.

Owen slowly made his way back to the lighthouse. As he approached, something red and gold caught his attention. It looked like a person's hair fluttering on the sea breeze. Upon closer inspection he saw the strands belonged to a woman.

She lay motionless on the rock. His mind reeled with concern. Was she injured?

Owen swung his gaze back at the departing *Rita Ann*. Perhaps the woman had been hurt by the same hands that piloted the boat. That would explain the hasty departure. Had someone on the *Rita Ann* dumped her there? Thrown her overboard? Owen's stomach twisted at the thought. Time was critical if that was the case.

He steadied his gaze on her, but from his vantage point all he could make out was her shock of long red hair, glinting with gold in the sun's rays. The tresses fanned out against the rock like the rays themselves. He leaned over the steering wheel as if that would get him closer faster.

With the engine of his boat chugging, he hoped she would hear him approach and lift her head or wave a hand, but she didn't. Not even when his boat sidled up to the rock and bobbed idly in the waves.

"Miss?" he called out over the rattling engine. "Miss, do you need help?"

No answer. No movement, either.

Owen cleared his throat and tried again louder. When that turned out the same, the words *deathly still* crossed his mind. Apprehension niggled at the back of his neck. He rubbed it and the horrid thought away and called out again. "Miss?" he yelled forcefully, but he couldn't deny the waver of uncertainty in his voice.

He hadn't seen someone this still since his wife, Rebecca, lay in the sand, paramedics going through the motions of saving her only because he begged them not to stop. Owen's throat filled with a golf ball–size blockage. He shot a jittery gaze toward the island, willing someone else to come help this woman.

The docks glimmered in the sunlight, waiting for his boat to find its place beside them for the night. Oh, how he wanted to do just that. To allow someone else better qualified to help her. He was good at chasing bad guys, not rescuing women. But not one person came into his view. Not one fisherman. Not one loitering teenager. No one at all stood on the pier for him to wave at for assistance.

Owen cut the engine. *It has to be me.* He dropped his shoulders as he dropped anchor.

He thought about radioing for help, but maybe the woman was just in a deep sleep. Just in case she was hurt, though, Owen grabbed the lifesaving equipment stored in the rear stern under the padded seats. He yanked open the compartment to find a first-aid kit and blanket, along with life vests. He scooped up the blanket and kit and went port side, reaching out to grab at the crusty barnacle-covered stone.

Swells rocked the woman in and out of his view. With every rise and sway of his boat, he caught sight of her one-piece red-and-blue bathing suit. He thought it was a mishmash of flowers or something but didn't concentrate enough on it to be sure. His full attention was given to the state of the woman's wellness. In a quick scan, his eyes followed from her bathing suit down her long, muscular limbs of milky white to a set of small feet sprawled motionless.

"I'm coming, okay?" he assured her loudly as he threw his load up on the rock and hoisted his body to follow. *Please be sleeping.* "Don't move. You may have a neck injury." *Like Rebecca when she was thrown.*

The woman didn't move. Not even to acknowledge his presence. He watched for any sign of a twitch or breathing as he scraped along the sharp barnacles. Pain sliced through his palms and bare forearms. He used the discomfort to propel him up and forward, but was glad for the protection of his denim jeans. Lying flat, he came face-to-face with the still, delicate features of the woman. Long, light lashes rested on pale freckled cheeks. He hesitated to touch her. Would he find her asleep? Dead? Had his rescue not come in time?

"Miss, can you hear me? Are you hurt? Do you need help?"

Nothing.

His hand reached for the curve of her neck and gently felt for her pulse on icy-cold skin. She moaned, and her heart's life-beating sound brought Owen a mix of relief and elation. She might be hurt, but at least she was alive. *Thank you, Lord,* Owen's reflexive prayer of thanksgiving had him wiping an old bitter aftertaste from his salty lips.

"God had nothing to do with saving this girl," he muttered. "God's not here. I'm here."

Owen reached for the scratchy wool blanket behind him and stretched it over her arms and chest to warm her. Instantly, her eyes flashed open wide and another short sound deep in her throat escaped her pale lips. A moan of pain? A quick jerk of her head triggered him to brace her in case.

"Miss?" He gripped both sides of her face and peered into stark gray eyes, as gray as the stone she lay on. Fear shone up at him. "Don't move. You could have a spinal injury. Can you tell me if you hurt anywhere?"

She struggled beneath the blanket, arms fumbling and pushing with a strength that caught him off guard. Owen pressed her arms down and shushed her. He couldn't safely move her to the boat like this.

She moaned again, more forcefully, louder. It didn't sound like a moan of pain now, but rather anger. She was mad at him? For helping her? She shoved harder at the blanket between them. Her lips parted for the loudest, most forceful sound yet. It sounded like the word "off" without the pronunciation of the *f*'s. It took him a second before her word hit him like a left hook to his gut.

Owen jumped away from the muffled sounds he would recognize anywhere. They were the same kind of sounds his son made when he tried to speak—ever since he'd lost his hearing the night he'd nearly drowned in the crash.

This woman wasn't injured at all. She didn't answer him because, like his son, she was deaf.

Miriam Hunter fumbled under the attack of a strong-armed man. The scare tactics to get rid of her had turned physical. Ever since she'd arrived, the islanders had made it known she wasn't wanted. First, the nasty notes and emails, then the late-night crank calls. And now this...this *assault*.

How dare this guy sneak up on her in this secluded place? The one place she could fully get away from their angry stares. As though it was *her* fault drugs had come to their precious island.

Just because the marijuana showed up after she arrived didn't mean she'd brought it with her. The bag of marijuana found in her office had been placed there by one of the very townspeople who wanted her gone—perhaps even by this guy leaning over her.

Angrily, Miriam heaved at the heavy material scratching her skin. She didn't have to think twice as to why he'd covered her with it. He might as well have sealed her lips with duct tape. She strained against him to free her hands—her voice. He wouldn't understand a word she signed, but it would make her feel better to put him in his place.

She wouldn't sit here and allow him to silence her. She pushed at him again, but his strength wouldn't relent.

Who is this guy? Miriam didn't recognize him as a parent. He seemed too young to have a child in high school. Thirty-two, tops. His dark cropped hair screamed military, not shaggy, salt-drenched fisherman.

But the eyes…

She stilled to study the rich black-currant irises inches from her face. Sharp and assessing eyes, not accusing and vindictive. She thought they held a message of caring, but before she could decipher it clearly, all emotion dipped behind their onyx surface like the secrets of the sea, safely hidden beneath murky depths.

His tensed lips moved, too close for her to read. Then as much as she abhorred talking, Miriam broke her vow and opened her mouth to tell him to get *off.*

The look on his clean-shaven face abruptly changed from determination to…shock? Her deafness surprised him? If he didn't know she was deaf, then he wasn't from Stepping Stones. He was a stranger—and she was alone on a rock in the ocean with him.

Every self-defense move Miriam had learned in college jumped to attention in her head. She tried to recall if there was a maneuver for when someone had you pinned under a blanket. Never did she think those tactics would be used, but perhaps this was the moment God had prepared her for through all those classes. *Stay with me, Father,* she signed her prayer of petition in her head because her hands were still secured under the blanket. *Give me strength and the knowledge to break away.* She mindfully pulled out the scripture tucked in her heart for times of darkness.

Do not fear, for I am with you. Do not be dismayed, for I am your God. I will strengthen you and help you. I will uphold you with my righteous right hand.

Miriam used the words from Isaiah 41 to hurl all her strength at the man again. This time, he jolted back as though she'd burned him. Without waiting another second, she sat up, flung off the blanket and scooted back.

He fell onto his haunches, hands raised in surrender, but her flight reflex still had her retreating farther away until she'd reached the edge of the rock. Her heart raced, pounding adrenaline through her head and body. Even being deaf, she could hear it coursing through her.

He hadn't moved from his place, but he spoke again. Miriam studied his lips as her breathing steadied. He said something about kelp. She shook her head in confusion and a bit of annoyance. People always thought deaf people could read lips. She supposed she could read them half the time, but that left a lot of room for error, which is why she usually traveled with her interpreter—except in the afternoon when she swam out to the lighthouse to be alone. Never did she think she would need Nick way out here.

The stranger's tall, lean frame bent to pick up a box labeled with the symbol of a red cross. He held it up to her and clarity came swiftly.

He hadn't said *kelp*. He'd said *help*. He thought she needed help.

But why? What gave him the idea in the first place?

Miriam searched the island and figured it to be about five hundred yards away. Not a huge distance for a former competitive open-water swimmer like herself. But this man wouldn't know she swam out to the lighthouse for exercise each day. He probably thought only a stranded and injured person would be this far from land.

Miriam supposed she could try to speak aloud to explain, but a long time ago she'd vowed only to use her voice when absolutely necessary. And giving this stranger her personal information wasn't necessary.

In fact, the only thing necessary was to get off this rock quickly. Miriam didn't believe she faced any danger from him anymore, but she also wasn't inclined to be friendly.

She cagily followed his movements to the other side of the rock, where his boat was anchored.

He gestured with his hand for her to climb in, pointing toward the island.

Before thinking, she naturally lifted her hands to sign. After the first few signs, stating she would swim back, she stopped and waved her hands to say forget it. He wouldn't understand anyway. She stood on the edge, still keeping him in her sight while preparing to dive in. But before her feet left the rock, Miriam glanced back at him one last time and froze.

His hand pointed to his chest, then rose to the side of his temple. She watched his index finger slowly point up toward the sky. "I understand," he signed.

She nearly stumbled over. He knew her language? Would he say more? She waited, hating herself because deep down she hoped he would. How quickly she willingly trusted this man just because he understood her.

For so long, though, she'd been a foreigner in this hearing world, desperately seeking companionship. Now she stood face-to-face with the one thing she sought. Forever on the lookout for someone like her, or someone who understood her. Or at least wanted to try.

Poor Nick earned his pay and then some. But there were only so many current events and prime-time television shows to talk about with one person.

Miriam knew her traitorous face was lit in anticipation of finding a friend, but even so she tried her hardest to be nonchalant about the situation. Tentatively, she raised her hands and swirled her fingers in circles. "You sign?" she asked in her language.

His eyes darkened to those murky depths again. He gave one negative shake to his head and averted his gaze past her shoulder.

He didn't sign.

Miriam did her best to express a lack of caring with a blasé shrug even though disappointment washed over her like a cold wave. Then her mind reminded her of the man's answer to her question. If he wasn't able to sign, then how did he understand her enough to answer her?

Unless he did understand her and didn't *want* to talk to her.

Fine…whatever. She dismissed him and his possible insult with a wave of her hand and lifted off the rock in one clean arc. Miriam sliced through the cold water with precision, letting it cool off her piqued temper, amazed her anger could still boil over so easily. She thought God had helped her with that unwanted emotion a long time ago, but sometimes her anger reared its ugly head and reminded her she still had some things to contend with.

Another day, she told herself…again. She wondered if there ever was a good time to reopen old wounds. She thought not, but especially not right now.

She was in the midst of a troubling drug investigation. She had a drug supplier to find. Making friends and digging into her past were at the bottom of her list.

In fact, her past was one thing better left buried. Nothing good could come out of unearthing those dreams—or rather, nightmares. Miriam trembled, and it had nothing to do with the frigid northern waters she swam in.

The unnatural bulging eyes from those old nightmares stared at her from behind her closed eyelids; a large hand and a flash of something gold blinded her. Images as real today as they were when she was ten years old. She pushed through her strokes as she pushed the childhood terrors down into the dark abyss.

Mother always said they were figments of a child's imagination. Except children weren't supposed to be imagining such horrifying things.

No, I can't go there. She swam faster, pushed harder. Her hands sliced through the water, propelling her forward. Miriam had a feeling if she continued to delve deeper into that nightmare, she would never emerge. Not even the dark-haired rescuer she left in her wake would be able to save her from the dangers of that dark and menacing grave.

TWO

"You really think the principal is your number-one suspect?" Owen waited with Sheriff Wesley Grant outside the high school's glass entrance doors. The buzzer signaled their authorization for admittance, and Wes pulled the door open.

"Her assistant's got a prior arrest for possession of marijuana," Wes discreetly informed Owen over his shoulder as they entered the school. "They neglected to share that little tidbit with the school board and don't know I uncovered it. I'm keeping it to myself until I have enough evidence for a search warrant of their homes."

"You seem to be putting all your efforts on these two. What is it about them you don't like?" Owen eyed a well-dressed man at the end of the corridor sweeping the shiny floors with an oversize dust mop.

"You'll see why when you meet them," Wes answered. "I feel like Ms. Hunter's constantly laughing at me. I'm a big joke to her." He sneered.

"Well, you are funny-looking." Owen jutted a chin

at Wes's head. "And you need a haircut, man. Have I been gone from Maine so long that the ladies dig the unkempt look now? Perhaps your principal is one of them. Maybe she isn't laughing at you at all. Maybe she's sweet on you. How old is she? Fiftyish?"

The green-clad sheriff chuckled. "Not quite." Wes pointed to a door off to their left. He cleared his throat a few times. "So, you haven't mentioned Cole since you arrived yesterday. How is your son?"

Owen's back tensed. "He's still living with Rebecca's parents over in Bangor. It's best that way. So, how do you think the drugs are getting here? This island's pretty secluded."

Wes nodded, taking Owen's cue. No more talk about Cole. "My guess is Ms. Hunter and her assistant have a connection with a Canadian drug cartel. They're helping to get the marijuana across the border by coming through my island. Then distributing it to their dealers on the mainland."

"But some marijuana was found on school property. Why release it and take the chance of shutting down their operation?"

"Well, that's where you come in. I need your, um, eyes to listen in on a few conversations."

"You need my *eyes* to listen? I don't understand."

The men reached the principal's office and entered. "Hey, Steph," Wes said to the cute, pixie-like secretary at her desk. "I'm here to see Ms. Hunter."

"Yup, she's expecting you." Steph lifted a slender arm rimmed with gold clinking bracelets and pointed toward the door. "She told me to tell you to go on in."

"Thanks, darling." Wes flashed a smile Owen thought might send the dark-haired girl into a tizzy the way she bloomed into the same shade of red as the netted lobster hanging on the wall behind her. Too bad for the girl if she thought Wes's flirtations meant anything.

Wes had cut women out of his life the day his fiancée ran off with another man. But unlike Wes, Owen had lost his girl by his own hand.

Twice in two days memories of Rebecca caused his stomach muscles to twist in guilt. He let the feeling remind him to never forget. She was so young and beautiful, glowing with that new-mother look that made him fall in love with her every time he watched her snuggle their son or every time she reached for him, honoring him with her complete and total trust. His jaded heart would swell over her pure one. She was genuine and didn't deserve to die.

But she had, and Owen had vowed to never ruin another pure heart again. Not another woman's and not his own son's. A solitary life would be his punishment.

"Uh, Owen," Wes held the door handle to the principal's office and spoke over his shoulder in a hushed voice. "There's something you need to know."

"What's that?"

Wes cleared his throat again, putting Owen on the defensive. Suddenly, the door opened from the inside, yanking Wes's hand along with it. Whatever Wes planned to say was cut off by a wiry-looking man, about five-eight, with blond hair and gold-rimmed glasses. Owen summed him up in two seconds as a nonthreat.

"Welcome back, *Sheriff.* We've been waiting for you." The man swept a scrawny arm wide to invite them in, but his tight-lipped words implied they weren't really welcome.

Owen extended a hand to the shorter man. "I'm Agent Matthews from the Drug Enforcement Agency."

The man eyed Owen's hand hanging in midair for an exaggerated second before placing his smaller, skinnier one into it. "Nick Danforth. I'm Ms. Hunter's interpreter. Where she goes, I go."

Interpreter? Did she not speak English? Owen thought Nick's response odd, but he shrugged it off. "Nice to meet you."

"Owen," Wes called from the front of the desk. A woman stood beside him, her hair twisted up loosely at the back of her head. Her slate-gray eyes grew wide as he leveled his own gaze on her. Even without the golden-streaked red hair flowing down her back, he remembered her from yesterday out on the rock.

She was the school principal? *And the number-*

one suspect? Could that really be true? A deaf principal in her early thirties didn't strike him as the drug-smuggler type. Yet he supposed he'd seen all types in his line of work and knew he needed to treat everyone as a suspect.

"This is Ms. Hunter. She's deaf," Wes announced matter-of-factly.

Owen caught Nick signing to the principal. *An interpreter for a deaf principal.* Nick's earlier response now computed. Nick shut the door behind them and sidled up beside Owen, ready to do his job.

Ms. Hunter raised her hands and signed, "It's nice to meet you, Agent Matthews."

"It's nice to meet you, Agent Matthews," Nick said from beside Owen, interpreting Ms. Hunter word for word. Only, neither of them knew Owen didn't need an interpreter. He understood her signs fine.

Owen turned away from Nick for a pointed look at his so-called friend. He could tell by Wes's prolonged stare and slight shake of his head that he wanted Owen to keep his sign language knowledge under wraps. *A little heads-up would have been nice.*

"I'll explain later," Wes said. "For now I would like you to get acquainted with Ms. Hunter and her staff so we can start the investigation."

Then it clicked why Wes had brought him there. Owen would be able to spy on what was said between these two when they thought no one else understood. If they really were the smugglers, then Owen stood a chance of solving the case pretty quickly.

Owen fisted his hands at his side. "You, too, Ms. Hunter," he said. Out of the corner of his eye he saw Nick translate his words to sign language. Owen continued, "It's my hope we can work together to get to the bottom of this problem on your island and in your school. I appreciate your help."

She visibly relaxed and her lips quirked up at the edges as she signed, "I want that more than anything."

"Grea—" Owen started and stopped, almost forgetting to wait for the interpretation. He deserved a swift kick for nearly giving himself away already.

"I hope you mean that," Nick translated.

I hope you mean that? What? Owen tilted his head and tried to figure out what he'd done wrong. He thought for sure she'd said she wanted to work together more than anything. Maybe his skills were rusty for lack of use. God knows he rarely used them. Having Nick might be a good idea, Owen decided.

He shrugged off his misinterpretation. "I understand I will be a teacher undercover. My goal is to find a leak that will lead me to the source of the drug supplier and then to the person smuggling the drugs to the island."

Nick signed as Owen spoke, staying at about three

words behind him. But Owen noticed Nick signed more than what was said. Owen recognized the extra signs as, "Don't forget. This guy is here to investigate us. Not to help us."

Ms. Hunter's lips twisted and a flash of humor sparked from her eyes. Then she signed to Owen, "I've made preparations for you to teach English in Mrs. Standish's classroom. She's out on maternity for another three weeks, so you'll be her substitute teacher. I'm hoping we won't need more time than that. Nick, stop translating. This is between us. I met Agent Matthews out on the rocks yesterday. He came to my aid when he thought I was hurt. I think he can be trusted."

Even though Nick stopped translating her final words, Owen kept on reading. He honestly didn't fault her for sharing their first encounter with her interpreter. He supposed he used secret codes in his line of work, too.

But never had he taught an English class in his line of work.

"Would there maybe be a gym class I could teach instead?" Owen asked. "Shakespeare never made much sense to me. Plus, teaching a class like that would take up too much of my investigation time."

"You and lifeguards," Nick signed to Ms. Hunter, ignoring everything Owen had said. "Just because a man comes to a swimmer's aid does not make him trustworthy. Your breakup with Lifeguard Andy should have taught you that lesson. Although I'm glad to see you're keeping the investigator busy and out of our hair. Your plan is brilliant. He's not too happy about teaching English, but he said fine."

Owen jerked. *That's not what I said at all.* Owen now knew he was not misinterpreting Ms. Hunter's signs, and he needed to inform her that her boy Nick was not translating correctly. But to do so would blow his cover and ruin any chances of "listening" in on these two and their conversations.

Wes believed Ms. Hunter guilty of covering up something. If sticking him in an English classroom had been her idea, Owen thought Wes might be onto something.

It was no wonder his friend had asked him to come all the way up from Texas instead of going with an agent from the Bangor field office or even Boston. These two were probably talking circles around him. Poor guy.

"It's a good thing, then, Agent Matthews isn't a lifeguard," Ms. Hunter signed. "Or I would be in trouble for sure." Her lips twitched again as she cast a glance at Owen. "Because he is not hard on the eyes."

Owen clamped his teeth together. It took every ounce of strength for him to pretend he didn't understand.

"Ms. Hunter says the English class is all she has

available, and I'm to show you to your classroom,"
Nick translated.

"Did she, now?" Owen bit the inside of his cheek.

"You can follow me," Nick mumbled.

"I was kind of hoping Ms. Hunter would join us
so we could go over the plan of action in more de-
tail." Owen directed Nick to ask.

Instead Nick signed to Ms. Hunter, "He's not your
type. And you better be careful what you say around
him. I think he's going to be harder to fool than the
sheriff."

Interesting. So Ms. Hunter was in fact fooling the
sheriff about something.

Owen searched her eyes. A mischievous twinkle
relayed that she definitely found something humor-
ous. Owen now understood what Wes meant when
he'd said she laughed at him. He was starting to feel
like the butt of a joke, too.

The lights flickered overhead.

"That's my TTY phone," Ms. Hunter signed to
Nick for him to translate information about her tele-
typewriter phone. Owen knew all about a TTY from
calling his son, but he kept quiet as she explained
through her interpreter. "It could be a parent trying
to reach me. No one on the island has a TTY machine to type their message into, so they have to use
a TTY service operator—a real live person standing by to take the caller's message and transcribe it
for me onto a screen. I can't keep them waiting, but

you go on," she signaled with a wave of her hand and then turned the machine to face her, pushing the button to answer.

Miriam hit the button to read the message as they were about to leave. When her pleasant eyes iced over, their steps halted.

Owen zoomed in on the screen, but she hit the end call button before he could read it.

Nick raced forward.

"What did it say?" Nick's signs demanded an answer.

Ms. Hunter shook her blanched face. "Not now."

"Tell me." Nick's refusal to take her lead had Owen paying closer attention to their words. His signing secret already proved to be beneficial.

Ms. Hunter's jumpy glances passed between Wes and Owen before she signed to her interpreter, answering his question. "Get off the island if you know what's good for you. Now go. We'll talk about this later."

"Another crank call? That's the third one this week!" Nick's hands slapped out, seemingly unconcerned with cutting the two hearing people out of the conversation...or so he thought.

"I said not right now." Ms. Hunter tilted her head toward Owen as she signed to Nick. Owen read the silent message loud and clear, but apparently Nick didn't. The guy's inability to keep his emotions at bay suited Owen just fine.

"It's got to be someone with a TTY so they can send you the message directly," Nick signed. "Using the operator service would be too risky. I'd give my right hand to know who on this island has one."

"Yes. Me, too." Ms. Hunter signed, then cringed. She studied her hands before continuing. "Well, maybe not my right hand. That would be like cutting out my tongue."

Owen understood Ms. Hunter wasn't worried about the pain of losing her right hand, but rather losing the only voice she had. It reiterated that his son would have the same hardship all his life—because of him.

Owen squinted up at all the diplomas and certificates hanging on the wall. There were a lot of letters after Miriam Hunter's name. He couldn't fathom how she'd achieved such great success. He didn't dare hope the same for Cole.

"I still think you should report these pranks," Nick signed quickly.

"Chasing pranks is not important right now." Miriam signed back. "Finding a drug supplier is."

"But what if they're related? What if this is more than an upset islander who thinks you shouldn't have this job?"

Owen tuned in to see what she thought about Nick's idea. Owen thought he was onto something. The only thing he caught was a spark of anger from Miriam Hunter's eyes. She apparently didn't like the idea of people thinking she wasn't worthy of her position. *But come on,* Owen scoffed. *A deaf principal for a hearing school?* She couldn't possibly do the job right.

"I think you should take that tour now," she signed with pinched lips. Nick's about-face out of the room made it clear the person in charge around here was Miriam Hunter. Her authoritative expression reminded Owen of his own adolescence spent in the principal's office.

But he had to wonder if her bravado was a cover-up for the fear he'd witnessed when she'd received that call. He hadn't missed the pasty hue that had marred her smooth complexion. Miriam Hunter feared someone or something. But why keep it from the police?

Unless she worried alerting them would bring something else to light.

Owen followed Nick and Wes and watched them take a left out into the hall. As Owen passed by the secretary's desk, he called out, "Give me a second, guys." He approached the desk. "Stephanie, right?"

"Yup. Can I help you?"

"Do you have a notepad I could use?"

"Sure." She pulled a pen from behind her multi-ringed ear and a notepad from her drawer. "Here you go."

Owen scrawled out a message for Ms. Hunter on the notepad and tore it off. The note included his cell phone number as well as an invitation to meet later to discuss how they could work together on the case. Buddying up might get her to open up, even if they had to spend the night writing everything down.

He stepped to the open door of her office. She had her back to him. Her folded arms pulled the back of her pale blue suit coat tight. She faced the window, looking out at the distant horizon of endless water beyond the rows of the fiery foliage. For a moment, her profile came into view. He could see her worrying on her lower lip.

Knocking would do nothing to alert her to his presence. Again he wondered how a deaf person qualified for a job such as this, and he thought of the prank call he'd witnessed. It very well could have been someone who thought her disability inhibited her from doing an adequate job.

Owen thought of his son and of his future limitations because of his deafness. Owen had to agree with the prank caller. He couldn't see how Ms. Hunter could perform her duties adequately. She obviously had the ability to fool a lot of people to get her position.

He stepped to her side, causing her to flinch. For a split second, Owen caught a glimpse of fear in her eyes. It retreated as quickly as the tide, leaving nothing but sparkles of wonder behind.

He'd never seen anyone so expressive before. She gave an elegant tilt of her head and an encouraging smile, and he could tell she was asking him what he wanted, even though she said not a word.

Owen handed her the paper, at a loss for words himself. A full smile blossomed on her face as she read the note. He wasn't expecting to see such joy— or to undergo the effects it seemed to have on him. His invite wasn't meant to make her happy, but for some reason he was glad it did.

A slender hand reached out toward him with graceful fluidity. It took him a second to realize she meant to touch him. Her hand landed with a slight squeeze on the arms he crossed at his chest. So much for a barrier. Alarm bells rang through his mind. Her touch felt like a branding iron leaving its mark on him. Owen belonged to no one. He couldn't. Not anymore.

He stepped back and gestured to the note. "Tonight," he said clearly, demanding that she read his lips and his body language.

She nodded as her countenance slipped to the same stunned look she'd had when she'd received the crank call. Good. She read him loud and clear. Let's hope she didn't forget it so easily.

Unlike Owen who could feel himself forgetting his punishment with each expressive thought she displayed on her upturned face. Her pale beauty and endearing freckles sprinkled across her cheeks made him think of sandy beaches on summer days. Her gray eyes washed over him with each cleansing bat of her lashes fooling him into thinking his sins could be washed away so easily.

Owen headed for the exit with quick steps. Speed became critical. He needed to close this case and get off this island before the charmingly beautiful principal made him forget his reason for being there.

Before Miriam Hunter made him forget his punishment permanently.

Lord, have you sent Owen Matthews to help me get to the bottom of the drug issue, or is he here to make me leave, too?

Perhaps she would have figured out by now who had placed the bag of marijuana on her desk if it weren't for people trying to scare her away. She felt the edges of her lips bend down and pressed them hard to rein in her emotions. Regardless of what the islanders thought, she cared about these kids and this school. And even this town.

Miriam straightened, breathing deeply. And whether they liked it or not, she wasn't leaving.

Not even for her dark-haired rescuer.

Miriam reread Agent Matthews's note. He wanted to work together. The idea of the two of them working side by side conjured up romantic images of late-night dinner meetings.

Stop it! This is serious, she told herself.

She blinked hard to get her mind back on track. Agent Matthews wanted to meet tonight. Should she cook? Or should they go to a more public place? The topic of discussion needed to be kept private from overhearing ears.

Miriam had an overwhelming urge to make her lemon chicken dish. She'd wanted to serve that since she'd come to the island. The thought of having her first guest elicited a spark of excitement. Of course, she never thought it would take this long, or that the first guest to sit at her table would be a DEA agent.

And a very handsome one at that.

Her hand still tingled where she'd laid it on his forearm. The sensation had surprised her, but it was the yearning to touch him again that really threw her. Maybe working together wasn't such a good idea after all. *I should do this on my own. I can't be losing my focus whenever Agent Matthews shows up. I might as well pack my bags and buy a ticket for the next ferry.*

Not willing to give up just yet, Miriam opened her top desk drawer and tossed the note in with the three other notes she'd recently received. She noticed how they were all written on yellow legal paper.

Agent Matthews's note didn't tell her to leave the island like the others, but she wondered if they all came from the same pad…and the same desk.

Stephanie's desk.

Miriam instantly disregarded that idea. Most likely every teacher in the building had oodles of these pads lying on their desks for someone to tear a sheet from. Following this line of reasoning sure wouldn't identify her threatening pen pal anytime soon.

Miriam reached for a student's file from the top of the pile on her desk. She'd been poring over any and all documented details about each student's past and home life that might point her in some direction.

Name: Colin Steady
Age: 16
Address: 285 Bluff Point
Parent/Guardian: Sam and Vera Steady

Miriam read through the past teachers' reports on Colin. All favorable descriptions of a boy who'd never had a detention and made himself at home on the honor roll. Always willing to lend a hand to teachers and help peers in their learning.

In other words, the dream student.

Miriam closed the file and moved on to the next.

Name: Deanna Williams

Wait. Miriam slapped the file closed. She'd been reading them in alphabetical order and knew of at least one student whose surname began with a *T*.

Ben Thibodaux aka Troublemaker.

She rustled through the remaining files. The final four of the full high school enrollment total of fifty-two. She checked her notes, counting the number she'd already explored.

Forty-seven.

I'm missing a file. Miriam hit the buzzer on her intercom for Stephanie. When her secretary failed to appear in the doorway, Miriam went in search of her.

She approached Stephanie's unmanned desk; the girl's opened diet cola had been left behind. The clock above the entry door read 3:40 p.m. Stephanie didn't usually leave until four o'clock, so she still had another twenty minutes to go. Miriam saw her secretary's coat hanging on the coat rack beside her own and Nick's. She was still in the building.

The girl had probably taken a bathroom break. Miriam decided to check the file cabinet and skirted around the desk to the cabinets lined up on the wall. She pulled the heavy metal drawer wide and flipped through each file, starting back with the *A*'s until she reached the end of the line with the *S*'s. The rest were on her desk, all except for Ben Thibodaux's.

A quick glance on Stephanie's desktop showed no sign of it there, either. Her gaze drifted to the cabinet beside Stephanie's desk. Her secretary considered it her personal drawer, so Miriam didn't want to open it, out of respect.

After another five minutes, Miriam walked to the hallway and peered down the empty expanse toward the faculty restroom.

She always carried a notepad and pen in her

pocket in case Nick wasn't with her and she needed to write something down to a person. She patted her right suit pocket to be sure the items were there and struck off down the empty hall.

Miriam reached the bathroom marked Faculty Women. Knocking would serve no purpose, so she pushed the door and entered, letting it swing closed behind her. The room contained two stalls, one of which was closed.

Mariam refused to speak. She hated speaking. She hated not knowing what she sounded like. She hated the looks people gave her when she tried. There had been a time when her mother and teachers had urged her to speak, even forced her to, but no one could force her now.

She crossed the yellow-tiled floor to the stall door and pushed on it. It opened easily. Empty. Stephanie wasn't in there, after all.

Miriam headed back to the door. She curled her hand around the cool metal handle and pulled.

It didn't budge.

She shook the handle a few times, wrenching it toward her, but no matter how much muscle she put into the pull, the door stayed shut.

Is it locked? But the door didn't lock on its own. It had to be locked with a physical key. A key that Stephanie kept on her desk. Had Stephanie locked the door for the night, thinking no one was in there? Wouldn't she have checked first to make sure?

Miriam pounded on the door. If Stephanie was still out in the hall maybe she would hear the banging and come back. Miriam fisted her hands and kept up the banging.

Please hear it, Stephanie, please! Miriam's words were only in her head. But in the next moment, the lights went out, and Miriam opened her mouth to speak aloud.

It was now necessary.

She hoped she was getting the words out correctly and loud enough for someone to hear. Her fists pounded harder. She fumbled in the pitch blackness for the door handle and yanked again and again. She banged and yelled some more. She banged through throbbing hands. She banged until they were numb. Someone had to still be there. Someone had to walk by sooner or later. If she let up, they would never know she was in there.

She pressed her cheek to the cool wood, feeling her drubbing vibrations pick up speed to a level of thrashing. Her heart rate joined the pace until sweat drenched her and she couldn't stand on her feet any longer. Her pounding weakened and slowed as her strength fizzled. She had no idea how long she'd been in there. It felt like at least an hour. Everyone was surely gone by now. Slowly she turned her back to the door and slid down to the floor.

Where was her dark-haired rescuer now? Probably down at the pier having dinner with one of the pretty local girls, laughing over something that wasn't even funny and making friends with people who could understand him.

Someone *not* like her. The freak, as Mother always said.

Miriam touched her face with pulsing hands and felt hot wet streaks of tears. She vaguely wondered when she had started crying as she stared off into the black room. She accepted she would be spending the night locked in this dark room as though she were ten years old again and being taught a lesson. And like all those other times of punishment, Miriam wasn't sure what she had done wrong this time to be locked away, once again isolated into a cold, dark world, when all she ever wanted was to find a home.

She closed her eyes, preferring the darkness behind her lids to the darkness around her. It gave her a sense of control in a situation where two of her senses were lost. Her hands moved by memory, calling on her heavenly Father as she had all those times of punishment in her mother's home. And once at her grandmother's when she'd come to Stepping Stones to visit with her mother.

That had been the worst darkness ever. So much so that Miriam, to this day, tried to block the horrifying images out, never wanting to relive the terror of that room in her grandmother's basement again. With its damp dirt floor and salty, musty air, it had been so much scarier than the closet at home. Her chest tightened. Pain ripped through her lungs from the remembrance. Images that could only have been the workings of her wild imagination still haunted her.

A woman with bulging eyes. A man's hand grabbing at her.

No one had been in that room with her. Mother had told her she'd made it all up. But if that was the case, why did it feel so real? So real that even though she now lived in her grandmother's house, she still refused to enter that room. It was locked, and it would stay locked forever.

Breathe, she told herself. *I'm not there now. I'm in a bathroom at school. Nothing scary here. Please, God, find me.* She leaned back and called on her true rescuer—the only one who could find her in the darkest of places.

THREE

The radio at Wes's belt chirped out a code that referenced a disturbance at the docks. "That's my cue to hightail it out of here." He headed for the classroom door. "I'll call you tonight to go over the plans for the impromptu locker searches tomorrow." He stopped in the doorway. "Oh, and Owen? Thanks for not being too mad at me for leaving out the fact that Ms. Hunter is deaf. I was afraid you wouldn't come if you knew. I know it's a tough topic for you...with your son and all."

Owen glanced up from his chair behind the teacher's desk. He could see that Wes was worried. "I'm over it." He hoped he sounded convincing and picked up the English class syllabus to change the subject. "Besides, the fact that Ms. Hunter gave me this intense of a class when I'm supposed to be investigating only makes me think you might be right about her. If the signing duo's guilty, their secret won't last for long."

Wes relaxed with a grin. "Great. I knew calling

you was the right thing to do. Good to be catching the bad guys with you again, buddy. See you tomorrow."

Owen jerked his head as a goodbye, but his attention was fully absorbed by the syllabus still in his hands. *It might as well be Greek.* He let the paper flutter to the desk. How was he ever going to teach this class? Why couldn't he be a substitute gym teacher or maybe a lunch aide?

He picked up a copy of the book the students were presently reading. *The Sonnets of William Shakespeare.* He hadn't been kidding earlier when he'd made that remark to Ms. Hunter about understanding Shakespeare. Apparently the jokes were on him now. He shouldn't be surprised she'd put him in this class. She was probably in her office now, laughing about it with her lackey.

Owen fanned through the paperback book, noting the number of poems that raced by on the flipping pages. "There's over a hundred of them. How am I going to pull this off?" he said, wondering if teachers could tuck cheat sheets up their sleeves. He made a mental note to make some tonight. He had to appear as if he knew what he was talking about, if for no other reason than to put the laugh back on Ms. Hunter.

After folding the syllabus, he stuffed it into the book and stood from his hopefully very temporary desk. He slipped the book in his back jeans pocket and hit the lights to the classroom.

The hall lights were all off except for red emergency lighting that lit up the corridors like a runway. He followed them back, turning at the corner of his wing into the main hall. The office door was sealed shut at the end of the long stretch. Had everyone gone home and left him there without as much as a goodbye?

What about his note to Ms. Hunter? Had she stood him up? All right, maybe stood up was the wrong phrase. That sounded too datelike, and a date was the furthest thing from his calendar.

He glanced at his watch; the red hue made it hard to read the little hand on the six. Through the glass entry doors, the last rays of sun filtered in, casting shadows on the walls and floor at the end of the hallway. Miriam Hunter and her sidekick were probably having dinner without him right now, thinking up ways to make his job harder. As if things couldn't get any harder than finding a drug supplier while teaching English.

Owen made his way to the exit. He didn't have a key yet, but he knew the doors would lock as soon as they closed. A jingling sound came from behind him. His rubber soles squeaked on the tile and echoed through the long empty hallway. He circled around, an ear tuned for the sound again. Something metal, if he wasn't mistaken.

"Hello?" he called down the hall. "Anyone here?" Nothing.

His hand went to his back for his concealed weapon. With his gun at his side, he took a silent step. His eyes darted to each closed classroom door. Anyone could be behind any of them. Any student could have hidden out after dismissal, waiting for an opportunity to make a drop or to get something in or out of the school while no one was there to see.

A door clicked behind him. Owen whipped around. The sight of Nick unlocking the entrance doors from the outside had Owen releasing his breath and reholstering his Glock.

Nick stepped inside, but didn't notice Owen standing halfway down the hallway. Owen cleared his throat to make his presence known. With a gasp, Nick grabbed at his chest in surprise. "Oh, man, you nearly gave me a heart attack. What are you still doing here?"

"Sorry." Owen walked toward Nick. "I was on my way out, but I thought I heard something. I was checking it out."

"It's an old building. It's always making weird sounds. You'll get used to it." Nick headed to the office and fumbled with a set of keys. When he attempted to insert a key into the doorknob, he missed the keyhole and dropped them to the floor with a clatter.

Skittish or clumsy? Owen debated while he

watched Nick bend to pick the set up and try again. "Hopefully I'm not here long enough to get used to it. But while I am here, could I get a key?"

"Oh, well, technically, I'm not authorized to hand them out. But under the circumstances, I'm sure Ms. Hunter won't mind me giving you one."

"Right, you're just the interpreter," Owen reiterated. The question Owen wanted to ask was: What else was Nick Danforth to the principal? "How can I reach Ms. Hunter? We were supposed to meet tonight. I have a few things I need to speak with her about before tomorrow."

"I'll give you her cell number. You can text her. Unless you happen to have a TTY machine."

"I do," Owen answered, but he wasn't about to elaborate, even with the dumbfounded look that appeared on Nick's face.

"Oh, I guess you came prepared, huh?" With a turn of the key, Nick unlocked the door and opened it in one clean movement. He flicked a wall switch and flooded the office with white fluorescent lighting, a harsh difference from the red emergency lighting in the hallway.

"I'll wait here while you write her number down." Owen stayed put, still wondering if someone else was in the building. He wanted to be in a place where he could observe if someone snuck out of one of the rooms.

Nick approached the secretary's desk and opened

a drawer beside it for a pad of paper and pen. "Well, I'll give them to you, but you won't be able to reach her right now." Hunched over the desk, he scrawled the pen across the pad in quick movements.

Owen stood in the doorway, his arms crossed at his chest, legs spread. "Why's that?"

Nick shrugged. "She left early tonight. She was gone after I returned from giving you the tour." His chin jutted at the coatrack. "Her coat's still here, but her car is gone."

Owen cast a glance at the lightweight blue Windbreaker. She'd probably figured it was warm enough and didn't need it tonight. But what was the rush that she didn't even tell her interpreter she was leaving? *At least it wasn't only me she neglected to bid adieu to.* "Is it normal for her to leave without saying goodbye?"

Nick tore the paper from the pad. "No, but the season for swimming is coming to an end. She probably wanted to get some exercise in before the sun set."

Owen nodded once, remembering he'd found her out on the rock about this time last night. Apparently it was part of her summer routine.

"I'll be right back with your key. Wait here." Nick unlocked Ms. Hunter's office and disappeared through the door. After a quick minute of sliding and slamming drawers, Nick reappeared with key and note in hand. "Here you go, Agent Matthews. I put my number on there, too, in case you need anything else. Anything at all."

Nick seemed much friendlier than he had earlier in the day.

"Great. Thanks." Owen turned to leave, pocketing the key and note in his jeans. "And, Nick, you should get into the habit of calling me Mr. Matthews. So you don't blow my cover."

Nick smacked his forehead. "Oh, man, I'm so sorry. I didn't even think of that. Good thing I didn't make that mistake with the kids around, huh? All right. I'll see you tomorrow, *Mr.* Matthews."

"Yeah, sure." Owen inched toward the exit, thinking something didn't feel right. Almost as if Nick was giving him the brush-off. As though he was in Nick's way. Owen pivoted to find the guy still in the office doorway. "Out of curiosity, what brought you back here tonight?"

"I forgot something." He thumbed over his shoulder, insinuating whatever he'd forgotten was in the office. "I'm gonna grab it and get out of here. Have a great night."

Owen didn't move, still not completely sure about the whole scene. "Where do you recommend eating on the island?"

"Eat? Um… The Blue Lobster on Main is great. There's also a German restaurant if you're into beer steins and lederhosen."

Owen smirked, picturing Hansel and Gretel Hummel dolls. "Nah, embroidered velour isn't my style."

"Yeah, me neither, but the pretty little aprons the waitresses wear are something to see at least once while you're here."

Owen nodded. "I'll make sure I put it on my list. See you in the morning."

"You, too."

Owen made it to the door and placed his hand on the metal bar to open it. As he pushed, the jingling sound he'd heard before sounded again. He scrutinized Nick over his shoulder. "Old building sound?"

Nick nodded, his face set firmly. "Old building sound."

Owen surveyed the hallway, peering into every dark corner the red lights didn't reach. Something did not sit right at Stepping Stones High. His hand dropped from the bar; he debated whether to check out the classrooms or to take Nick's word.

Seriously? He inwardly scoffed that he'd even considered the word of Nick Danforth.

Owen backed away from the bar and strode away from Nick, who in Owen's estimation was becoming more weasel-like with each passing moment. "I'm gonna check the rooms out anyway."

Nick scurried out of the room to come alongside Owen. "Is this really necessary?"

"Nick, I'm here to investigate a crime, so I would say yes, this is necessary." Owen opened the first classroom to his right and flipped the light switch. A scan between desks turned up nothing.

The same for the next two classrooms.

"There's no one here," Nick said from behind Owen. "See? Nobody. Nada. Nothing but an empty school." Nick's voice rose an octave with each word.

To alert someone, perhaps? Owen eyed Nick more closely. "Why do I feel like you have something to hide?"

"I'm not hiding anything," Nick huffed, and exited the classroom. He went to the next room and opened it himself. He continued to expose room after room, flicking lights on to prove his innocence. "Like I said, no one is here."

Owen had to agree, but that didn't mean he wouldn't be digging a little more into who Nick Danforth was and where he'd come from. But for tonight, Owen had exhausted his search, and there was nothing left but to go home and continue his investigation in the morning.

They walked back down the hall, classrooms closed up tight once again. "What time do you arrive in the morning?" Owen asked.

"I get here at seven. Ms. Hunter is usually here—Hey, now where ya going?"

Owen had noticed a closed wooden door he hadn't checked behind yet and he bisected Nick's path to cut across the hall. He pushed on the door marked Faculty Women, but it didn't budge. Locked. "Where's the key?"

"I guess on Stephanie's desk, but I don't know why she locked it. The bathrooms aren't usually—"

"Just get the key." Owen cut off his rambling.

"Right."

Owen gave the handle two more yanks out of impatience while waiting for Nick to return.

A thudding sound came from behind the door. Owen stumbled back in surprise. More banging alerted him to the fact that someone was on the other side. "Who's in there?" he shouted over the rising noise.

No answer. Only more banging.

"Please, calm down and tell me who you are." Owen turned his head and hollered down the hall. "Hurry up with the key, Nick. Someone's locked inside."

Nick came running out of the office, searching for the correct key on a ring of many. "Here, try this one. I think that's it." He thrust the keys into Owen's hand and Owen inserted one into the lock.

With the person on the other side, he couldn't push through as he wanted to. The person was obviously distressed. "Move back so I can open the door," he instructed, but it didn't help. The pounding continued. Was it a student who'd been left behind?

Owen pushed in a little, hoping the person would see the door opening and move out of the way. With the door ajar, he saw no light coming through. The poor thing was locked in the dark. He spoke through the crack. "You're all right, but you need to let us in to help you." He pushed a little more and suddenly the banging stopped.

Owen could now hear snippets of a voice. Little squeaks, followed by a moaning much like the one he'd heard yesterday.

Miriam.

"Miriam!" Nick said it in the same moment Owen thought it. The smaller man elbowed Owen out of the way. He succeeded, but only because Owen allowed him to pass.

With no other lighting besides the red backlight, Owen could only make out the outline of Miriam clinging on to Nick for dear life. Obviously, he was someone special she went to for comfort. He was more than an employee to her.

"Bring her out here." He held the door open to allow Nick to guide her out of the dark. Owen walked behind them down the hallway, listening to Miriam's sobs muffled in Nick's shirt. Each sound squeezed his chest and built in him a need to reach for her as Nick had.

It wouldn't take much to push Nick aside. Owen gave himself a mental shake. The direction of his thoughts confounded him. What was wrong with him?

He put himself back on the task of figuring out

how Miriam had gotten locked in the bathroom in the first place. How long had she been in there? Was it Stephanie who'd locked her in? Had it been an accident? Or another, more daring, prank? And why were the lights off?

How did Miriam bear that?

Her sobs quieted to murmurs, but Owen thought perhaps she hadn't borne it very well at all. He wondered when she'd given up hope of being found for the night, and thought of Cole and how his eight-year-old son needed to sleep with a night-light. The dark posed more than the absence of light to him. It meant he was silenced. It meant he didn't exist anymore.

Owen followed the two into the office and watched Nick gently put a disheveled Miriam in a chair. The hair that had been twisted up in the back so neatly a few hours ago now hung in thick, teased clumps around her shoulders. No trace of the earlier humor in her eyes remained.

Nick reached his hands out to hold her face and to pull her attention to him. His thumbs gently wiped her tear-streaked cheeks. He knelt in front of her and signed to her slowly. "You're okay now. I've got you. No one is going to hurt you anymore. This is going to stop now. If you won't call the police, I will. You understand?"

Miriam didn't reply. She looked over at Owen with red-rimmed eyes full of fear. The fact she didn't hide it now twisted Owen's gut. He took a step closer to her, not sure what he meant to actually do when he reached her. He wished more than anything the mischievous twinkling would fill her eyes again.

That *he* could be the one to restore it.

Focus on the case, Matthews. This was not an accident, and you need to figure out how it's related.

"Are you sure her car is gone?" he asked Nick, trying to put the pieces together. He remembered that tidbit of info Nick had told him earlier.

Understanding of where Owen was going with that dawned on Nick's face, and he nodded emphatically. "It's not in the parking lot. That's why I thought she'd left."

"Then someone stolc hcr car."

Miriam inhaled sharply as her head shook back and forth, her face a mixture of different emotions. Shock, denial and disbelief paraded across it. She obviously had read his lips accurately. She jumped to her feet; her words sped so fast her hands tripped over each other. "Someone stole my car? This is crazy! I have never done anything to the people in this town. Why do they want to hurt mc like this?"

Nick began to translate, his voice filled with deep sadness, projecting the pain she felt with each word. He obviously knew her well enough to know her words were not filled with anger. Owen wondered how deep their relationship went—and why he cared.

He backed a step away, reaching for his cell phone to put his mind on a different, more innocuous, track. "I'll call Wes to report the stolen car," he announced. "How far could it go on this island, anyway? I'm sure we'll find it."

At the same time Owen would find out who was behind the threats and put a stop to them. Because there was only one thing worse than being responsible for destroying a pure heart.

Not protecting one.

FOUR

"The breaker to the bathroom was shut off." An elderly custodian stepped into Owen's classroom, moving at a snail's pace and hunched so far, Owen thought he might topple right over. He shuffled to the chair beside Owen's desk and plopped down into it.

"As in *someone* flipped the switch." Owen closed the Shakespeare book and tossed it onto the desk. He'd studied it as much as he could. Any more details would fall out of his head now.

"Exactly. I would say someone meant for Ms. Hunter to spend the night in the dark." He offered a hand to shake. "Len Smith."

Owen eyed the man carefully before taking his hand. A hint of an accent on the man's lips caught his attention. German, maybe? "Owen Matthews. Nice to meet you, and, yeah, I would say the same thing. You wouldn't happen to have any ideas, would you?"

"Me? No, but I'll be sure to keep a watchful eye

out for any more deviant behavior raised against Ms. Hunter." Len shook a crooked finger. "Her grandfather and I went way back." The man cleared his throat, hacking away while Owen watched to be sure he would survive the spasm. "Hans and Trudy were good people. They would be heartbroken to see their only granddaughter treated so harshly, especially by someone here on Stepping Stones."

"When did they pass away?" Owen took the opportunity to sneak a backdoor peek through the screen of Miriam's life. For the case, he told himself, but that didn't explain the tentacles threading around his larynx. Owen rubbed absently at his neck.

"Trudy died two years ago, but it's been about ten years now since Hans went on to his eternal home. He was a bit younger than me, but a good friend."

"If you don't mind me asking, how old are you, sir?"

"Ninety-one years old." Len's chest puffed with pride.

"And still working? That's amazing." Owen wondered why but refrained from asking.

"Nah, Alec lets me push a broom around so I still feel needed."

"Alec?"

"Alec Thibodaux is the head honcho of custodial engineering." Len cackled. "Not a day goes by he doesn't remind me that he's in charge. I just remind him that I still sit on the school board and write his paycheck."

Owen appreciated Len's laid-back manner. "Likes to throw his weight around, does he?"

Len smiled and waved a gnarled hand at Owen's comment. "He's a good guy, and one swanky dresser."

"Oh, I think I saw him yesterday when I arrived. I'm glad he lets you help out around here."

"Yes, well, regardless of what happened to Ms. Hunter last night, Stepping Stones is made up of good people. We care about each other."

"Apparently not everyone feels the same way."

Len's bent shoulders fell in more. "I hate to agree with you, son, but you might be onto something there."

"Can you think of any reason why someone would target her?"

"Funny how you sound more like a cop than an English teacher." Len's eyes twinkled.

"Why? Is my prose a little rough around the edges?"

"Just a tad."

"Will I be able to fool the kids, you think?"

Len waved a hand. "You'll be fine. Kids don't pay much attention to adults. You must know that from your own kids, right?"

Owen floundered in his answer, not sure what the older gentleman would think if Owen told him it was the other way around for him. That it was the adult withholding the attention.

"Oh, sorry, Mr. Matthews. I just assumed you were married with children."

Owen's gut twisted at the mention of marriage. "I was once." He swallowed with a gulp. "My wife died."

Len's head bounced in understanding. "Ah, me, too. Death is hard, but it can be even harder for the people left behind. I guess all we can do is honor our loved ones who have passed on, huh?"

"Yeah," Owen whispered. He let the pain of his guilt fill his chest once again. How could he have allowed himself to forget her so easily? To forget he'd taken his son's mother away from him? Because of golden-red hair blowing in the breeze? Because a pair of amused gray eyes had weakened him into thinking he'd been punished enough? Was that it?

Well, no more, he scolded himself. *Locate those drugs, find the source and get off this island.* That was the plan he would stick to.

"Mr. Matthews," Len's voice rasped. "How do you suppose one goes about honoring those loved ones?"

"By not allowing yourself to forget," Owen ground out.

"Nope." Len sighed with a shake of his head. "You honor them by picking up your broom and pushing on."

* * *

Miriam edged to the side of the door so she could observe Agent Matthews's class through the long, thin window without giving herself away. Students sat at their desks; some sprawled across the tops, while others passed notes. One of them even slept.

Perhaps she should reconsider Owen Matthews as a substitute English teacher.

Originally she'd thought it would be beneficial to keep him busy. But that was before last night. If it hadn't been for him, she would have spent the night on the floor of that dark bathroom alone. Was he there to bring about her demise or to help her?

Miriam changed her position enough to bring him into her peripheral sight. He stood at the chalkboard, scrawling out Shakespeare's sonnet "Shall I compare thee to a summer's day?" She'd always liked that poem and its reminder that every life has value and wants to be remembered.

Miriam knew she wasn't being very nice putting Agent Matthews in this class. She sure wasn't valuing him by setting him up to fail. She placed her hand on the doorknob but waited for Agent Matthews to finish writing before interrupting his class. He might not be reaching the kids at the moment, but disrupting his teaching could cut him down even more in the students' eyes.

Agent Matthews dropped the chalk on the ledge and rubbed his hands together as he faced the class.

Thinking this might be a good time, Miriam turned the knob to enter, but a hand gripped her forearm and yanked her back before she could.

Startled, Miriam swung around to find Nick. Eyes emblazoned with anger stared back at her. "What's wrong?" she signed.

"What's wrong?" Nick's hands slapped out. "How about the fact you can so easily forget that man is here to get you fired. I know what you were about to do—give him an easier class. I can see it on your face. How can you roll over after everything you've done to get to where you are?"

Miriam peered back through the window. Agent Matthews had come around the desk to prop himself on the edge; his arms were folded across his chest. His white dress shirt stretched tight across his wide back. He smiled at something someone said. A dimple dented his clean-shaven cheek.

Miriam's breath hitched at the sight, and she immediately lost her focus. Flustered, she dropped her hand to her side and stepped back from the door.

Nick was right. How could she forget so easily? Her life was an uphill battle to prove she had value. She was not some dumb mute. She couldn't let people forget that. She had to wipe out any obstacle in her way.

Especially the handsome dimpled ones that made *her* forget.

* * *

The school bell rang, and the students raced for the door without a backward glance. Owen had no idea if he'd connected with any of them. He circled his desk and grabbed the eraser to wipe away the poem. Words that expressed Shakespeare's vow to remember someone in his life. A promise to honor the memory for all time.

Rebecca filled his mind, and Owen viciously wiped away the chalked words. *So long as men can breathe or eyes can see / So long lives this and this gives life to thee.*

What had Owen done to keep Rebecca's memory alive? He'd taken her pictures down because he couldn't bear to look at them anymore. Did that stop her image from haunting him anyway?

No.

He couldn't speak about her to her own son without guilt weighing on him. Did that mean Cole didn't want to know about her?

No. It only jammed more of a wedge between him and his son. It only piled more guilt onto the stifling amount that existed.

And it only made Rebecca's life less significant. As though she'd never existed in the first place.

"Mr. Matthews?" A voice yanked him from his torment.

He cleared his throat as he cleared his mind. "Yes,

what can I do for you? I'm sorry, I don't know your name."

"Ben Thibodaux."

Owen focused on the boy's face and remembered him sitting at the back of the class. Ben's double silver disc earrings sparkled from his ears, in contrast to his dark and dull clothing. His black painted lips matched his eyeliner. This kid must really irk the quaint people of Stepping Stones, Owen thought, but he withheld his judgment for the time being.

"Any relation to Alec, the janitor?" Owen asked.

"He's my uncle, and he doesn't like to be called that."

Owen nodded. "I'll remember that. So, let me guess. Billy Shakes gives you the shivers, and you need help? Am I right?"

The kid hesitated, scanning the hallway of passing students. Did he worry about getting caught actually talking to a teacher? Would that ruin his reckless image? "Yeah, you could say that. The thing is, I need to pass this class," Ben said.

"You and everyone else."

"Yeah, but I need to graduate and get off this island. Otherwise—" Half of Ben's lower lip disappeared behind his upper teeth as it became gripped in their hold. If he bit down any harder, there would be blood. Owen came around the desk and propped himself against the front, a foot away from Ben. He gripped the edge of the desk as he waited to hear what Ben wanted to say.

"Otherwise what?" Owen urged him forward.

"Otherwise I won't have anything to look forward to but a life of doing someone else's bidding."

Owen crossed his arms. "Whose bidding?"

The stark look of fear crossing Ben's face had Owen holding his breath. Was this his lead coming to him already? Was Ben Thibodaux his link to the drug distributor?

"I gotta go." Ben backed away, then raced for the door. "I'm gonna be late for my next class."

Owen followed on his heels. "If you need to talk to me confidentially, you can. Remember that," he managed to get out before Ben escaped the room, running right past Miriam and Nick. Owen disregarded them to follow Ben, but the boy disappeared through the crowd. One second he was there, the next, gone.

"I need to see his file," Owen said with his back to the duo. Out of the corner of his eye he saw Nick translate.

"You can't have the file," Nick replied.

Owen whipped around to face the principal. "Why's that?"

"The file is gone," she signed, and Nick interpreted.

"What do you mean the file is gone?" Owen's words were pronounced so slowly, Miriam didn't need Nick to translate. The agent's tight, pursed lips and his dark, accusative stare said he thought she was keeping information from him. No doubt her ploy at assigning him an intensive class to teach had lost her a few points in the credibility department.

At a time when her credibility mattered most.

The man was there to investigate her. What had she been thinking? He was a federal agent, not a small-town sheriff.

It had seemed like a good idea in the beginning. Keep him busy and out of her hair while she did her own snooping around. Except here he stood, leaning into her, close enough to smell her cherry blossom shampoo. She might as well get used to it.

Miriam waved a hand to move them back into the classroom and away from young, intrigued eyes.

Stiffly, Agent Matthews reentered the room, his gaze still riveted on her. Miriam instructed Nick to interpret while she signed. "Regardless of what Sheriff Grant has told you, I am not the bad guy here. I care about this school and want these drugs gone from this island as much as he does."

Heavy scrutiny filled his eyes. "Then give me the file."

"I don't know where the file is. That's what I was looking for last night before I got locked in the bathroom. I noticed it was missing when I was searching through each student file." Her hands stilled for a moment. "May I ask why you want the file? Ben has had some trouble in the past, but I don't believe he's dealing drugs. Unless you have some type of evidence I should know about?"

Agent Matthews's lips moved too quickly to read and Nick translated with the typical lag. Miriam kept them both in her vision, going back and forth between the two men's faces. A disjointed way of living, but necessary to survive and succeed in this world.

"He just seems like the type to be involved in criminal behavior." Nick signed the agent's words.

Miriam shrunk back, unsure if she read the signs correctly. "What a horrible thing to say!" Eyes flashed and red blotches colored the agent's checks. Miriam wondered what *he* had to be angry about. "Do you always judge people by their looks when carrying out your investigations?" Miriam demanded.

Agent Matthews squeezed his hands together, his face mottled with suppressed rage. He looked like he really wanted to say something and struggled to hold back. Perhaps he was mad that she'd called him out on his prejudice.

He said nothing, though. His chest heaved. His lips sealed tightly as his gaze darted to Nick.

Miriam made up her mind that tomorrow she would give him the world history class to teach, as well. *If* she couldn't get rid of him sooner. "I don't think you're the right person for this job, not if that's the way you carry out your work. I have these students to protect, and I think you should leave." Miriam pointed to the doorway, leaving her hand extended in the air.

He stepped closer, tripping her up for a second. Miriam pushed herself to her full height, eye level with his chin. He paused in front of her. She raised her chin a notch while his gaze held hers. Miriam stomped her foot and pointed harder at the exit.

It did nothing to move him along. What it did do was cause his lips to curl up ever so slightly. She could have sworn his black eyes softened on her. Before she could assess if that was the case, the dark ire they'd held a moment ago flashed defiantly back at her. He didn't say anything. Not one part of his body moved. His message was as clear as her stomping foot.

He wasn't going anywhere.

It seemed getting rid of Owen Matthews was going to be harder than she thought.

"I want everything you have on Nick Danforth in my hands. *Now.*" Owen spoke to Wes on his cell phone in the warm cab of his rusty borrowed pickup. Wes had set him up with the truck, and at the moment it was the most secure place to make this phone call, even with the scorcher of a day. He just couldn't take the chance of being overheard.

The students were eating lunch in the cafeteria

at the moment. Owen had a reprieve from playing professor. He was due back in forty-five minutes for a freshman class on writing a thesis statement. He remembered enough from school to know what it was—simply stating what you believe and what you intend to prove.

"Nick Danforth is our guy," Owen said into the phone. *Now only to prove it.* "I just witnessed the interpreter pull the wool over his boss's eyes. She had no idea he misinterpreted what was really being said. The only person who can tell if an interpreter is getting the message right is another interpreter, and he wasn't getting it right—on purpose. He made me out to be some judgmental bad cop when I only wanted more information about a particular student as a potential lead."

"Are you sure this wasn't another one of their games, like the ones they played on me?" Wes's voice held a high level if irritation.

Owen scanned the parking lot. The sign for the principal's parking spot stood two spots down. An old vintage Vespa parked there. Its bright blue finish showed its age in rust. Apparently Miriam had another set of wheels. Owen found it difficult to picture her zipping around on it. He wiped a hand across his forehead. "You were smart, Wes, to ask me to come. Even if you didn't tell me up front about Miriam's deafness."

"Like I said, after everything with your son, I knew you wouldn't have come if I had."

Owen sighed heavily and took another swipe. Sweat came away on his palm. He had to be perspiring because of his anger at Nick or the warm interior of the cab, or both. It couldn't be from the guilt that kept his son a stranger to him, and definitely not from the fiery redhead who'd just stomped her foot at him as though he were nothing more than another bug to be squashed in her long line of grievances.

The smile he'd held in check in her office broke free now. The woman was full of surprises. She sure didn't act like a disabled person. The twinkling mischief and laughter in her eyes demonstrated her quick wit and smarts. Nick couldn't misinterpret that no matter what words he changed. He also couldn't misinterpret the way she went to bat for Ben Thibodaux. She was a woman secure in herself and her position and apparently her deafness.

He wondered what her secret was—and if she would share it with him. Maybe…just maybe… He pushed the far-fetched idea aside. His son would never be so lucky.

"Leaving out the fact I would need your signing capabilities for this case was a necessary omission," Wes's voice broke into Owen's aching wish for a normal life for Cole.

A bead of sweat trickled down the center of Owen's back. It was too hot to sit in this truck. He pushed open the door and headed for the back parking lot where the tree line would give him the privacy he needed to continue this conversation. He spoke as he walked. "I'll admit I was caught off guard for a minute yesterday, but as soon as they started talking I could see why you needed me. But Wes, I got to tell you I think Danforth is our guy. Not Miriam."

A strange odor wafted to Owen's nostrils as he reached the trees. He paused to survey the forest before him. Dense foliage of blazing reds and ambers was difficult to see through, but he did notice that no birds chirped in the autumn stillness.

Too still, he thought, and the feeling of being watched pricked the hairs on the back of his neck. Owen stepped past the tree line to enter the woods. Old fallen leaves from years before crunched beneath his feet. Only a few trees had let their leaves go so far this season.

Owen sniffed and placed the odor. He didn't need a mechanic's license to know the sharp smell of gasoline. From where he stood, it was close by.

Wes rattled on about Nick's run-in with the law ten years ago. Owen listened on in silence while he continued to survey the area. He reached out to a few broken branches, noticing more like them ahead.

Something large had come through there.

Owen knelt to the ground to lift leaves, scattered loosely about. Not old, packed-down, decomposing leaves, but freshly fallen leaves—and a whole bunch of them. In his estimation, it was too many for this early in the season. And they were only in this area.

He lifted a chunk away, exposing the old earth beneath. A few more swipes and he had what he was looking for.

Tire tracks.

"What kind of car does Miriam have again?" Owen cut Wes off.

"An old maroon Dodge. It belonged to her grandparents. She inherited it with the house."

"Does she have any other family here?" The question slipped out before he could stop it, but Owen justified it as background information and good to have. He scanned up ahead, where the lay of the land dipped down. A ditch perhaps?

"Nah, not anymore. The Hunters only had the one daughter. Keira Hunter was a wild one, according to my parents. Ran her own parents ragged and then ran away to the mainland. Showed up a year later with a baby in her arms and no husband." Wes made a *pffing* sound. "Women," he finished with disgust in his voice.

Owen ignored his friend's last retort and focused on the interesting info about Miriam's mother. Where was Keira Hunter now? "So did Miriam grow up on the island?"

"Nope, just a few visits. Whenever Keira got evicted or something. You know how that goes.

From what I know, the last visit Ms. Hunter had here was when she was ten years old. After that, she wasn't seen or heard from again until the reading of Trudy's will."

Owen loomed closer to the drop-off. "How did Miriam get the job?" That was one question eating at Owen. "How does a deaf person qualify for a principal position? Especially one who doesn't live on the island already?"

"You and everyone else want to know. The school board made the decision behind closed doors. My guess is it's because of who her grandfather was. Hans, Len and Frank came here together after World War II."

"Frank? I've met Len. Is Frank still around?"

"Yes. He's the youngest of the trio—eighty-six, I believe."

Owen reached the edge and halted, seeing exactly what he expected. "I found the car."

"Uh-uh," Wes said.

"Uh-huh," Owen replied. "Maroon Dodge. Looks like it was driven through the backwoods of the school parking lot and pushed into a ditch."

"Well, Ms. Hunter could have done that. This doesn't prove anything."

"I don't see what she would gain. Besides, she was locked in a bathroom."

"So she says. I'm coming over." Wes disconnected and Owen pocketed his phone.

Gasoline fumes burned his eyes. He surmised that the tank must have been damaged in the car's trip down the ditch and now leaked out everywhere.

Owen circled around the vehicle, then approached it from behind. The rear seats were empty and so was the front. He found the driver's side door unlocked. He scanned inside for a clue as to who might have taken the car and dumped it there.

A few white candy wrappers littered the passenger floor. Saltwater taffy wrappers, from what he could tell. He imagined Miriam's favorite flavor was spiced apple. A little sweet and a little spicy to match her personality. But if that was the case, then his flavor would have to fall under sour apple.

A *Simple Hospitality* magazine rested on the passenger seat. Brand-new with a label addressed to Miriam Hunter, 555 Cliff Top Road.

A gold piece of jewelry lay on the floor.

These items didn't mean anything. All of them could belong to her. It would be impossible for him to know if something came from the car thief. He would need her to give him an inventory so he could tell if something was missing or added. He also wasn't holding his breath that the perp had left a calling card.

A distant popping sound echoed through the woods, jolting through the car. Owen recognized the sound as a gunshot. He was being shot at? Backing out of the driver's side door, he crouched low to use the car as a shield.

Then he remembered the leaking gas.

The shot was not meant to hit him. It was meant to hit the empty gas tank—empty except for flammable fumes. The farther away the shot was made, the more heat the bullet gained to ignite the tank full of fumes.

Owen rushed for the embankment, hitting the base in the same moment the car exploded behind him. Air whooshed from his lungs as he landed facedown. Heat burned his back while blackness loomed over him. He struggled to get in a breath of the smoky air. His body wouldn't move no matter how much he willed it to. An image of Cole flashed on the backs of his eyelids.

I can't die. I've never told my son I'm sorry. I've never told him I love him.

Owen forced his head up, using the image of his son to propel him forward. Only, the face staring back at him over the embankment and through the haze of smoke wasn't Cole's.

It was Miriam's.

Heat closed in on Miriam in all directions. She pushed through the burning of her eyes and face to make out the person lying on the hill. Her eyes focused through the haze. She inhaled a sharp breath of smoke.

It was Owen Matthews.

Was he hurt? Escalated panic had her stepping sideways to try to reach for him. Owen lifted his hands and signed, "Get back! I don't want you to get hurt. Go!"

Miriam backed up to the outside heat barrier, filling her lungs deep with air that wasn't so thick and noxious. She pulled her cell phone from her pocket and sent a text to Nick. Fire in backwoods of school. Call 911.

Miriam dared not leave Owen down there. Why he was there she couldn't fathom, but neither could she fathom how a fire would start out here. When she'd seen the flicker of flames from her office window, she'd thought it was her imagination.

Mother always said her imagination was in overdrive, always seeing things that weren't there. Miriam figured she should check it out before she alerted the authorities. Most likely it was the brilliance of the fall colors swaying in the breeze. But this was a real fire and, if she saw correctly through the flames, that was her car in the inferno.

Another prank gone horribly wrong? Or a message of danger directed at her? With Owen possibly hurt, it felt like the latter. And where was he, anyway? She watched with eagle eyes for him to appear over the edge.

She used the lapel of her suit coat to cover her mouth while breaking the barrier of heat again. She couldn't stay back any longer. What if he passed out from the smoke? She had to get him out regardless of what he'd said...*or had he signed it?*

Her face burned from the heat, but Owen was in the crux of the blaze. It didn't matter how he'd spoken. Or that her throat burned from breathing in the scalding fumes as she disregarded his command and went back in. It didn't matter that she could feel the hair on her head singeing against her scalp. Miriam had to get Owen out. That was the only thing that mattered.

The black smoke thickened; she couldn't see a thing through her gritty eyes. Something grabbed her foot. Miriam bent to feel a hand reaching over the top of the ditch; smoke billowed out behind it.

Lord, help me. Provide me Your strength to help Owen. She drew on the promises of God to help her pull Owen up and away from the flames and smoke. *Lend me Your righteous right hand.* She heaved with all her might until his foot came up from the edge and he fell to the ground.

She reached for his upper arms and tried to drag him, but he was so heavy. Words for him to move were on her lips, but in her panic, she couldn't be sure if they were correct. He got to his knees, his shoulders drooping as he signed, "Get back—it could blow again."

Definite signing.

Miriam pushed the revelation aside and signed,

"Not without you." She reached for his arms again. This time she was able to drag him a few feet across the forest floor. At first Owen stumbled in her arms, dragging his knees. "Move!" she yelled and hoped it came out correctly.

He pushed himself up to his feet. She led him to the clearing and toward a parked car. They reached a blue minivan, diving behind it just as the pressure of a huge explosion smacked her in the back, sending her flat to the ground with Owen.

He hacked and coughed; his body lay facedown, while his shoulder blades jerked with each wretch. Concern for his well-being swamped her as she felt each spasm beneath her hands. She fisted the cotton fabric of his shirt in her grip, realizing her arms were around him. Her gaze dropped to the arm he'd thrown across her, then followed lower to where half his body lay over her. He'd used his body to shield her from the blast.

Had he been as concerned for her safety as she was for his?

In his state of spasm, he could say nothing to her. But a few moments before, Owen had spoken to her. Technically, he hadn't said one word. Instead, he'd raised his hands and signed to her as plain as day. His signs held no hesitancy in them. They were clear and purposeful.

And fluently accurate.

Miriam dragged her attention from where his leg

covered hers and stopped at the hand on her shoulder. The hand that had spoken to her with expertise, then pushed her down to safety. His own fists balled the material of her suit in them, clinging on to her as she was to him. He hadn't just pushed her down. He'd grabbed hold of her with every muscle beneath his skin and refused to let go.

His jerky movements from the coughing lessened. Miriam drifted her muddled focus to a pair of black eyes ensconced in a black-soot face. His adrenaline-enlarged pupils penetrated through her, scrutinized her. She could see the worry on his face. Worry for her safety? Or worry that he'd given his secret away?

Did he know his cover had been blown?

Why would he keep his knowledge of sign language from her? Why use the interpreter at all? *Oh, please, Miriam, you know exactly why. Owen was sent here to investigate you.*

His hand came away from her shoulder. It should have relieved her from feeling restrained, but instead she missed its weight. It implied safety, even when the truth was he only meant to earn her trust so he could do what he'd come there to do.

Determine if she was guilty.

With her hands freed, she pushed herself up to a sitting position and raised them to speak. His charade would stop now. She would make it known she knew. "The fire department should be here soon. You should probably go to the mainland to be checked out in a hospital. All we have here is a clinic." Her signs picked up speed, giving him no breather, but by the way no confusion crossed his face, he didn't need it. "Do you know how the fire started?"

Owen pushed himself up on one elbow. His lips moved. He looked to be shouting, but not at her.

She whipped her head around to find Nick and Sheriff Grant approaching from the other side of the minivan. Owen had been calling out to them, not answering her. If he understood her, he wasn't telling.

"Are you all right?" Nick signed to her while he spoke out loud to Owen.

Owen nodded with his eyes locked on her. He raised his eyebrows. Was he silently asking her if she was all right, too? Or was he asking her to keep his secret? To do so would mean being dishonest with Nick. She'd never kept anything from him.

Owen's lips moved, and Nick resumed as her ears. "He doesn't want to be treated," Nick signed. "He wants the car and woods secured for inspection and the school under lockdown. He thinks there might have been a shooter."

A shooter? He had to be mistaken. Miriam searched the tree line and turned back to Nick for more information.

But Nick stopped translating. His hands froze in midair while Owen continued speaking.

Miriam waved at Nick to continue. She hated

being cut out of a conversation. Her gaze hopped between the two men, trying to read lips and get caught up. She needed to know what Owen was saying.

Nick sighed heavily. His shoulders rose and fell before his hands began to move. "You're not going to like this," Nick signed to her. "He says from now on, you will not be out of his sight. Day and night."

FIVE

Young faces plastered against every available window surface. The students of Stepping Stones High had probably never seen such a spectacle in all their teenage years. Nor had the seasoned teachers, either, for that matter.

Owen followed Miriam as she headed toward the building with her interpreter by her side. The weasel had sure fooled her. Owen sneered at the back of Nick's neatly combed blond hair, each strand perfectly in place. He portrayed himself as a real wholesome boy. How much of it was a farce? Did Nick misrepresent the truth of his identity as he'd misrepresented Miriam's words? Owen wondered what he would have to do to prove Nick's slight to her; then he thought of how she'd withheld the knowledge of Owen's signing capabilities from everyone, including Nick. Perhaps she had a reason not to trust Nick, either. Something to look into further for sure.

Regardless of Miriam's reasons, though, Owen had his own. Something told him he didn't want the deceitful interpreter knowing his signing secret just yet. Not until he could clear Nick of any wrongdoing in the case. The lying to his employer was a whole other matter. He would let her decide what to do with that tidbit on her own.

Nick reached out to hold the door for his boss. It all seemed very casual and the common way of things. Owen imagined Miriam depended on Nick for a lot more than his interpretation skills. He was sure there weren't any other people on the island who signed. That probably made her life really lonely. If there was nothing romantic about Nick's relationship with her, it was at least a tight friendship. Owen felt a little bad for what he was about to do.

But only a little.

The students in the hall made a path for them. Shocked and drained faces stared back at them. Someone threw out the question, "What happened?" A deluge of inquiries and comments spurted forth as the kids gained confidence to speak freely.

"What started the fire?"

"Are we in danger?"

"Can I call my mom?"

"My parents are going to flip!"

Miriam stopped, her head held high along with her hand to halt them. Owen knew she couldn't hear them, but she must have sensed their fear and urgency. He stepped up beside her as she began to address the students in her language. The expression on her face had him transfixed.

It was the face of a leader.

Her eyes softened on the students, reaching out to them with a sense of comfort and understanding, but also a sense of dedication. She would protect every single one of them with her life. And her words told them so. "I want you all to know there is nothing to fear at your school. But right now, for your own safety, the school has been put under a level-two lockdown. I need you to stay in your classrooms while the police and firemen do their job of putting the fire out and inspecting the woods for any further harm. Your parents will be called in a few moments. Teachers, please take your students back to your classrooms. Until we know what happened, please keep them there with blinds drawn and doors locked. I will make the rounds shortly and let you know when the lockdown is lifted. And please keep them safe."

Nick addressed the crowd. His words started accurately enough, but he soon put his own spin on her message that ended with, "Everyone back to your class. Teachers, you should know better than to allow the students to be out in the hall. You need to follow the correct protocol for times of risk and danger. Don't let it happen again."

"Hmph." A teacher off to Owen's right made the sound. He twisted his neck to catch her scrunching her pudgy lips in distaste at Miriam. "That's all she has to say?" He heard her say to another teacher under her breath. "I shouldn't be surprised she doesn't care. It's not like she's one of us."

The other teacher nodded; her glasses slipped to the tip of her nose and angry eyes flashed above the gold rims. "Let's go, students. You heard what she said. Get back to class."

Slowly the students turned their frightened stares on their teachers and allowed themselves to be corralled back to their respective places. One by one, they filtered out of the halls; doors were pulled closed. Some with soft clicks, others not so much.

At the end of the hall, two people stood in the dim shadows. Owen squinted and noticed their black clothing. One was a girl from his first period class. She had her arms crossed over her chest and leaned against the lockers.

The other was Ben Thibodaux.

Even though the boy was all the way at the other end, Owen could feel his leveled stare on him. But Ben would have to wait.

"Hold up," Owen called to Miriam and Nick as they entered her office. Miriam kept walking, but Nick stopped and turned back. "I need you to stay out here for a little while. I need to speak to Ms. Hunter alone."

"Alone." Nick smirked. "And just how do you plan on doing that?"

"Steph, do you have that pad of paper again?"

"Oh, sure, Mr. Matthews." Her bangles clinked away as she pulled her drawer open and removed the yellow legal pad. "Here you go." She flashed him her cute smile.

"Perfect. Thank you." He took the pad and directed Nick to sit in one of the waiting chairs. "I'm going to need to talk to you also, so wait there."

"Sure, that's fine. Plus if you need me to interpret, I'll be right here."

Owen stepped into the room and shut the door behind him. Miriam stood behind her desk, looking not at all surprised that it was only him who entered. He walked up to her desk and tossed the pad on it; the top few pages fluttered like a flapping sail in the wind, then settled still. He wasn't going to need that, and they both knew it.

Owen lifted his hands and signed, "Your interpreter is a liar."

Owen's remark tripped Miriam up, but only for a second. With impactful hands, she signed, "The only person who is a liar is you! You've been lying to me since the first moment I met you. I directly asked you if you signed, and you said—"

"I know what I said. I said no, I don't sign, and it's the truth. I don't, but I do understand it."

"You're signing now."

He regarded her quizzically. "I guess I am." An

expression of wonder crept onto his face. His eyes implored her as though she had the answer as to why. "With you, I don't seem to have the same problem."

"Who do you have a problem signing with?"

A simple question, but he either wasn't going to answer or it wasn't as simple as she thought. She tilted her head, the fight in her evaporating. She came around to his side and took the seat Nick usually sat in. With a wave of her hand, she invited Owen to sit. She hoped her choice in seats would make it more comfortable to share.

But he didn't move. His legs braced apart. His blackened arms crossed at his chest. He was as formidable as the stepping stones. A staunch protector of the secret within him. She'd thought the secret was that he could sign, but apparently there was more.

"I won't tell. Promise." It wasn't too often she made a promise like that, but every now and then a student would need reassurance before they would fess up. She tried to picture Owen as a young schoolboy, his hair rebelliously long. His eyes darkly defiant, much like the students she faced off with in her office.

She always wondered why it took so long for them to realize she wasn't the bad guy. That, in fact, she was on their side. She only wanted what was best for each and every one of them. No matter how many times she said that to the people of Stepping Stones, she still met resistance. Like she did with Owen.

And he wasn't even a local.

What was she doing wrong? She had to wonder if Mother had been right. Maybe she was too much of a freak to belong anywhere. "I thought Stepping Stones would be a place I could call home," she signed. "I have a few happy memories from when I visited my grandparents. Even with them gone, I thought it would be like it was when I was young." She shook her head and let her gaze drop with her hands to her lap. She squeezed her palms together before she continued. "But I was wrong. No one trusts me, and all I am met with is—" she swirled a hand in his direction to insinuate his seditious stance "—this."

Owen's arms dropped to his side. A shamefaced expression replaced his previous noncompliance. He took the chair beside her and settled on its edge. "I'm sorry."

She waited for him to elaborate, raising her eyebrows in question.

"I have an eight-year-old son. He's deaf." Owen looked across her desk, away from her. "I have trouble signing to him."

Miriam hadn't been expecting that. Owen had a son? She checked his empty ring finger. She shook off the direction of her mind. Why it even veered that way she didn't know. Stumped, she sat in silence. She processed his reason for withholding this information a few moments ago. His defiance hadn't been because of her nonacceptance into this community after all. It had been out of his shame for having a deaf son.

She didn't know what was worse.

"My mother refused to sign to me, too," she admitted, hoping her pain wasn't obvious. But maybe she could show Owen the error of his ways before his son paid the devastating price of a life of silent solitude.

"I didn't say I refuse to sign to him. I said I— Never mind. Forget I said anything." His jaw ticked, and he exhaled deeply. "Do you really want to know why you don't fit into this town?"

She straightened in her chair. The very question had been at the forefront of her mind since she'd arrived. She shrugged a single shoulder. Could she get any more noncommittal?

"Your pal, Nick, isn't relaying your messages accurately. His translations aren't even close to what you're saying. He's been painting you as the most vicious man-eater on Shark Week."

Miriam locked her hands together as her head shook. Nick wouldn't do such a thing to her. He was her best friend. Her only friend.

My only friend. The thought repeated over and over. Was there a reason he was her only friend? How long had he been doing this—this highly unethical practice for an interpreter? Owen had to be lying. He had to be.

She searched his face but saw nothing but remorse. And not the lying kind. Instead, his expression said it hurt him to be the one to raise the bad-news flag. Bad news that unfortunately made sense. From day one, Nick had set her up to fail.

Miriam stood and marched to the door, her blood boiling to the point where she could cook a lobster. She gripped the doorknob and pulled.

The door didn't budge.

A look to her right confirmed why. Owen had come along beside her and stopped the door with one of his strong, lean hands. She latched her gaze on to the simple barricade as though it was the first hand she had ever seen. These appendages allowed her to move forward in life, but this one now stopped her in her tracks.

He faced her, inches away. So close she could feel the heat of his breath on her cheek. A turn of her face brought his soot-covered lips into her view. They moved and she recognized the silent word on them as *no*.

He gently covered her hand on the doorknob without letting her gaze go. His thumb rubbed over the back of her hand, bringing confirmation that he meant no harm in his blockade.

But she had a few choice words for Nick on the tips of her fingers.

Owen's piercing dark irises softened on her, and the heat from his hand dulled her anger.

Her hand fell away from the door still grasped in his hand. Miriam curled her fingers around his and squeezed with the real emotion bubbling at the surface.

Pain.

Then the first tear fell.

With his other hand, Owen pulled her head to his shoulder, massaging her as her weeping face nestled into the side of his neck. His rough afternoon stubble scratched against her cheeks and forehead. The abrasiveness didn't compare to how broken and raw her heart felt at the moment.

Growing up with her mother had toughened her to people's doubts in her capabilities, but that didn't make it hurt less.

But the pain would have to wait. She had major cleanup duty to take care of first.

With her eyes still downcast, Miriam broke away from Owen knowing what she must do before more bridges were burned. Nick's time here on Stepping Stones was over. She would think about the end of the friendship later. Her duty as principal came first.

"I have to fire him," she signed with her head bowed to hide the pain the very idea caused her. This stranger in front of her wouldn't understand that she wasn't just firing an employee. She was losing her best friend.

Owen's hand brushed her cheek so tenderly she barely flinched under his unexpected touch. Miriam knew he was trying to get her attention. She strained to compose herself before listening to what he had to say. Even though she wasn't crying anymore, she still ached.

He lifted her chin, not waiting for her to find her legs to stand strong. Owen forced her to look into his normally critical eyes. The judgment she expected to find from the serious law enforcement officer didn't match the compassion she witnessed. Perhaps he did understand the pain of losing a best friend.

His hand cupped the side of her face. She waited for him to pull away so he could speak to her, but the language he used now didn't need words. The expression in his eyes told her more than enough. They told her he understood.

She turned her face into his palm and signed, "It hurts."

He nodded once, then dropped his hands and stepped back. His posture changed from understanding to passive indifference. "It doesn't matter if it hurts," he signed in quick, jerky movements. "Nick can't know. I think he's guilty in more dealings than misrepresenting you."

"The drugs?" The shake of her head denied what Owen was saying. "No. He wouldn't be involved in something illegal like that."

"He has been before."

"What? When?" She squinted in confusion.

"About ten years ago he was arrested for possession."

Stunned, Miriam grasped at the possibility that Nick might be involved in the drug problem. She wanted to deny what that meant. If he was responsible for the drugs getting on the island, then she, too, was responsible. She'd brought him there. If it hadn't been for her, Nick would never have set foot on any of the stepping stones.

She thought back to how he'd almost decided not to join her in Maine. Even raising his pay hadn't made him jump on board right away. She tried to think back to the day Nick had texted her, saying he was in. Had he given a reason for the sudden change in plans? She didn't think so. All she could remember was her own elation that Stepping Stones was going to be her home. With an interpreter to help reconnect her with the people she remembered from her childhood, she'd believed there was no way this replanting of roots could fail.

Except it had.

Owen waited for her compliance. As gentle as he'd been with her a moment before, she knew if she wanted to disobey, his request for her silence would become an order. With his feet firmly planted as they were, she read his message loud and clear.

Her hands were tied.

But even if they weren't, she would do whatever

it took to uncover the truth. Miriam nodded and signed, "Okay. You have my complete assistance in this matter. I brought Nick here. If he is the supplier, then I have a lot to make up for to these people. The retribution for their injustice is more important than my retribution for the pain he has caused me."

Owen's jaw set; his dark eyes became lethal. "No," he signed with sharp movements. "Not more important. Just as important. You'll have your day, Miriam. I promise you. You'll have your day."

SIX

Miriam accelerated her Vespa around the bend in the road. The view of the endless ocean would appear as soon as she exited the thick forest of back roads leading to her home. More than ever she wanted to hit the waves and swim out to her lighthouse no matter how cold the water. In fact, the colder the better. She imagined the frigid waters numbing her core and easing the pain from Nick's proverbial knife in her back.

Miriam hoped it wouldn't be long before she could fire Nick. It would be so hard to have him by her side day by day, but she resolved not to let Nick's betrayal hurt her anymore.

She gave her scooter more gas, feeling the vibration of the motor under her seat. A feeling she remembered experiencing as a child when Grandpa Hans took her out for a ride on it. A memory Miriam relished with joy, because it reminded her that Stepping Stones was not a place she'd dreamed up. Her few visits here had really happened. All the images from those visits were real memories, not whimsical illusions of a lonely girl.

Miriam broke through the forest into a clearing and caught a glimpse of her home sitting high up on the cliff, looking out over the sea in all its splendor and glory. An old ship-captain's home with a widow's walk perched on the rooftop. Its gray clapboard siding and white trim needed a fresh coat of paint and the roof was missing some shingles, but for the most part, Miriam had inherited a real gem.

The offers to purchase since the reading of the will conveyed that. A few times she'd hesitated in her refusal. Maybe she could take the money and go buy herself a place in the world. Except deep down she knew that would take a lot more than money. She knew what she needed were roots—like the roots her grandparents' home offered. The fact that the principal job opened up shortly after the reading of the will made it feel like an invitation to come home and claim those roots as her own.

Out over the watery horizon, the sun said its last goodbyes as Miriam zipped along with the cliff's edge on her one side and the conifer-filled forest on her other. Her home sprang up at the end of the winding road right before it dropped off into the wide-open sea.

As she neared her house, a pickup truck parked out in front caught her attention. Miriam slowed and flipped up the tinted visor of her helmet to identify it as Owen's rented truck. She'd seen him park near her in the school parking lot that morning. Not that she'd been waiting for him to arrive or anything. She'd just happened to be looking out her office window when he'd pulled up.

Miriam wondered why he was at her home now, then realized she hadn't informed him of her leaving school. After the horrendous afternoon of convincing parents the school campus was safe and the fire was a lone incident, Miriam had craved some solitude.

Owen couldn't have been serious about her not leaving his side. She would need to tell him she could take care of herself. She didn't need a babysitter. Not to mention, his idea was preposterous.

The truck's headlights turned on and it drove toward her. The fact that he couldn't sit tight and wait for her to reach him said he probably had a lot to say and she wasn't going to like any of it. Miriam pulled over and braced herself for the tongue-lashing, or more like the hand-lashing, she was about to receive.

She smiled and bit her lower lip. She wouldn't admit it to his face, but it was nice having another person on the island who spoke her language. Even if he was about to yell at her.

Miriam lifted her helmet off her head and let her hair flow freely. She trailed her fingers through her hair, then paused when the truck's speed exceeded past common sense out on this cliff. She kicked the bike stand down to prop the scooter up and straddled over it.

The truck propelled forward even faster. Miriam's stomach rolled in apprehension. Something didn't feel right. Almost hostile, even. But that couldn't be the case. Owen wouldn't harm her, would he?

The idea that he might have a dangerous streak made her queasy. She swallowed hard and watched the truck careen around the curve of the cliff, coming closer at its ridiculous speed. Miriam lifted her foot over the bike to get off. When the truck veered across the road and entered her lane, her escape became fumbled.

Owen was going to hit her! The idea was unfathomable, but she didn't have time to think it could mean anything else.

Miriam stumbled back, realizing she wouldn't be able to get out of the truck's path fast enough. She flung her helmet into the street for a blind dive off the edge of the road and down into a patch of prickly trees and brush. The smack of hard earth ricocheted through her bones, but even so, she pushed herself into a roll to get farther away from the road. A solid tree trunk ended her momentum with a jolt. Her lungs ached as all her air expelled in a rush. Stunned and bleary-eyed, she struggled to sit up and scan her surroundings.

Her scooter remained parked. From her position, Miriam couldn't be sure if Owen was still on the road or if he'd driven away. She was sure he'd meant to hit her, though.

She could feel herself gasping and forced her body to relax enough to refill her lungs deeply. She would need air to think clearly in case Owen came back.

Owen.

Tears pricked her eyelids. She did not want to believe he could ever be so cruel. So dangerous. She needed to call the sheriff, but with the two of them being friends, that line of thinking could be futile. Especially if it was the good sheriff who'd brought Owen here to scare her off in the first place. Maybe it was Sheriff Grant sending all those notes…and maybe it was Owen who'd blown up her car. It would explain why he'd been down in that ditch.

Determined to find out, Miriam pushed her body up to stand, but her ankle gave out from under her. She nearly went back down, but hunched over to balance her weight before she could.

A sprain, she told herself, while she became aware of all her sore places screaming out. A burning feeling came from her legs where her skin was scraped—her long skirt and silk stockings were not the best protection.

Miriam didn't think any bones were broken, but she assessed each of her movements carefully while slowly gaining her feet. She pushed her hanging hair out of her eyes and swept a shaky hand down her face. Stickiness pulled her attention to her palm—smeared blood covered her hand.

She was hurt in too many places.

A sudden feeling of vulnerability overcame her.

Miriam shot glances up and down the empty street. The truck was gone. And so was the sun. *I need to get out of here,* was her only thought.

Miriam stuck to the safety of the trees as she made her way to her house. She wondered, though, if she was moving at all. It wasn't more than a thousand yards, but with cut-up legs and a sprained ankle, every step posed a challenge, especially with her head pinging back and forth from front to back. She wasn't able to hear if someone was behind her—or coming back for her.

Pain shot from her ankle, and Miriam inhaled with a wheeze of breath through her clenched teeth. She needed to get off it for a minute. She leaned against a tree to inspect it in the growing darkness. A pine needle protruded from her ruined silk stockings. She plucked it out as headlights appeared down the road. She pushed through the pain and raced around the tree to be shielded from view.

The only reason to come out this far was to come to her house. For seven months now, she'd wanted nothing more than for someone to visit her. No one ever came, so she didn't believe for a second this visitor was looking to chat it up over coffee.

The longer and lower shape of the vehicle told her

it wasn't Owen's truck. She waited for it to reach her, but it seemed to be moving slowly. It stopped a few times. She thought maybe the driver knew she was in the woods—knew because they'd witnessed her dive into them.

Miriam stilled and plastered herself to the tree, not daring to move as the car crept by on the other side. She turned her head, waiting and watching for it to pass.

Only it didn't.

The car stopped right behind her tree. Her fingernails bit into the hard bark of the trunk as she wrestled with what her next move should be. Miriam couldn't tell if the person was still in the car or if he approached her. There would be no way for her to know until he was upon her. Not unless she peeked her head out to look.

She had two choices. Try to run home and make herself known, or run deeper into the woods. Either way, she was going to have to run. She couldn't stand here all night playing hide-and-seek behind a tree. If someone wanted to find her, a tree was not going to protect her for very long.

Dear God, I can't do this by myself, and I have no one to call for help on this island. I have never felt so alone...so isolated...so scared. Not even in the darkest of closets. I know You were there with me then, and I know You are with me now. I'm stepping out because I trust You to see me through to safety as You always have. See me, Father. Hear me, Father.

Miriam stepped straight into the dark forest, putting distance between her and the car on the road. With each step she fought the need to look over her shoulder to see if she was being followed. In the next second, a beam of light gleamed off the tree in front of her.

She had her answer. She was being followed, and whoever it was had a flashlight.

Miriam frantically picked up her pace, weaving through branches and trees. The bouncing ray of light grew bigger and ensconced her surroundings. It told her he was right behind her. Her upper arm flung back when something grabbed her. Miriam cried out in fear and frustration at being caught, but the grip on her arm triggered a past lesson to resurface automatically.

In one swoop, Miriam whipped around and banged her fist into the wrist that held her. The force loosened her assailant's hold, giving her enough time to slam her palm up into his nose. The flashlight went flying above her, blinding her for a second before it landed behind her and settled its beam on… Owen.

He stood before her, holding his nose, his other hand up in surrender. But that didn't make her want to stick around. Miriam stepped back to run again.

"Wait. Don't run," he signed, halting her. "What

happened out on the road? Were you in an accident?"

Miriam's chest rose and fell. She didn't answer him, but stood still and silent, trying to decide if she should trust him or not.

"Are you hurt?" Owen stepped closer, and Miriam retreated a step. "When I heard you had left the school without me, I ran to the parking lot and found my truck gone. I was so afraid—" His signing stopped in midair. His exploring eyes assessed her face.

Miriam wanted to believe more than anything that Owen wasn't in that truck earlier. She thought if he was, then he was a good actor. His concern for her felt sincere. But if it wasn't him, then she was back at square one.

She noticed him squinting. He couldn't see her very well with the light shining on him and not on her.

She picked up the flashlight to put them both into the light. She searched his face for any clue that he might be lying. Any twitch of a smile at the sight of his handiwork on her face. Or raised eyebrows in mock surprise.

Instead his face twisted in confusion, then morphed into anger.

Or fake anger, she reasoned, and signed, "If you thought you could run me down to make me leave, you thought wrong. I'm not going anywhere."

"Run you down?" Owen signed with genuine shock on his face. "Is that what happened?" He reached out again.

Miriam yanked her arm away before he could make contact. "Yes. With your truck." She stepped back on her bad ankle and winced a bit before she masked her pain from him.

"You're hurt," he signed. Apparently her masking capabilities were lacking.

"I'm fine," she signed.

"No, you're not." He clenched his teeth before he continued signing, "Who wants you off this island, and why?"

She couldn't give him an answer. Saying it was him who wanted her off the island didn't feel right to her. Especially with real anger radiating from him. It didn't feel faked. The fever look of his eyes cut into her resolve. She could feel herself swaying to believe he hadn't been behind the truck's wheel. Did she dare let it melt her distrust in him?

"Someone wants you off this island for a reason," he continued more slowly, his rage contained. "It's stopping you from doing your job. Don't you want to know why?"

Miriam hesitated before she nodded her answer.

"Then let me help you find out."

Air rushed out of her lungs. She hadn't realized she'd held her breath. So afraid and alone. Owen's offer beckoned to her better than any lifesaver float.

But should she trust him?

Did she have a choice?

He spoke her language.

So had Nick.

"How do I know it wasn't you who ran me down?" she signed before making her decision.

"I promise you it wasn't me. But if you need more proof than that, I was still at the school when you left. Check with your fire chief. I just left him."

"I don't know who I can trust," she signed.

Owen unclipped his phone from his waist and thumbed out a text. He hit Send and gave her the phone.

Miriam read the text he sent to the fire chief, asking what time he'd left him. A moment later the phone vibrated in her hand. The reply read 6:30.

Less than fifteen minutes ago. There was no way Owen would have been able to run her down, return to the school to switch cars and get back to her and be in the chief's presence at the same time.

"It wasn't me. Now will you let me help you?" He reached for her elbow with a gentle hand.

Miriam nodded tentatively, but then made her mind up and leaned her weight onto him. Relief flooded her as the pressure was taken off her foot. She squeezed her eyes through the pain and let him guide her out of the woods and back to the road.

Up close she could see the car he drove was a deputy's olive-green cruiser. He held the door for her, all the while assessing her every move. Definitely not someone who meant her harm. She felt comfortable with her decision and she relaxed back into the seat as he came around to the driver's side.

He left the overhead light on so they could sign.

She lifted her hands and said, "Do you always drive a cruiser when you're undercover?"

His cheeks blotched as if he'd realized his slipup. He slumped forward and smiled. "I guess I wasn't thinking. All I cared about was finding you. I grabbed one of the deputy's cars still there from the fire." One shoulder rose in a short shrug as he put the car into gear. "I guess I was worried."

He was worried about her? She processed that as he drove the remainder of the way home. Miriam overanalyzed his reaction to death. But how often did a law enforcement officer let his decisions take a backseat to their instincts? Probably not too often, she figured. Not unless a feeling for a certain individual overpowered their senses and caused them to act irrationally. She gave herself a mental pinch to curb the direction of her thinking. Owen Matthews was not interested in her. He'd given her no indication that he thought of her in any way other than platonically.

A memory from the day after she'd met him flashed into her mind. Something she'd said…or signed. Something about him not being hard on the eyes. The words she'd signed to Nick resurfaced.

Miriam inwardly cringed as she realized Owen had understood her perfectly that day! Every word.

Her stomach flipped as a laugh rumbled deep down inside. She pressed her lips tightly to hold it in, but her shoulders couldn't be contained. They shook with abandon.

"What's so funny?" he asked with one hand as he drove toward her house.

There was no way she could hold it in any longer. Miriam let the laughter burst forth from her lips. "I'm sorry." She tried to sign; her fist at her chest swirled in a circle motion. It was all she could say to his perplexed expression.

"What's so funny?" he signed again with one hand.

She tried again. "I just remembered what I said to Nick the day after we met, when I thought you couldn't understand sign language."

His eyes narrowed, apparently not grasping her meaning.

"I signed that you were easy on the eyes. It just hit me that you understood all that."

His face split into a wide grin. His heart-melting dimple aimed right at her. Miriam breathed the sight in deeply. Easy on the eyes didn't come close to describe the level of magnetism she felt luring her in.

Owen gave his nose a quick rub before signing. "Speaking of hitting, where did you learn to hit like that?"

Miriam giggled again, signing. "Oops, sorry about that, too."

"A smile is a smile in any language," Owen signed in the dim light of the car's interior. "The meaning of that phrase just hit me."

Miriam tilted her head, her brilliant smile changing to one of serene beauty. "Please, no more hitting." Her lips quirked at the edges as she smiled.

He thought she might laugh again, and he waited expectantly for the tinkling sound to fill the vehicle.

He wasn't sure why he wanted to hear it again. He also couldn't describe the shift taking place inside him, either. He just knew it had something to do with her smile. One simple gesture that said more than any word she could have spoken or signed.

Her smile meant acceptance.

Owen exited the car and reeled speechlessly around the front of the cruiser. Struck mute by this offering because he didn't deserve it.

He'd messed up. The car fire had conveyed a dangerous warning he knew was meant for Miriam. Pranks had escalated into threats against her life. He should have seen this coming. He shouldn't have let her out of his sight. At the school, when he'd realized she'd left without him he hadn't been able to get here fast enough. Then to come around the corner and see her Vespa and helmet in the road... Owen swallowed a growing lump in his throat just thinking about the ideas that had raced through his mind.

The main one being that he'd arrived too late.

Owen didn't think he'd breathe another breath while he'd searched the tree line for life. Her life. Hoping he would find her in the trees and not sprawled on a rock below the cliff. When he'd caught movement in the growth, it had offered him a spark of hope.

Maybe he wasn't too late.

Owen pulled open the passenger door and saw Miriam's torn tights and bloodied legs.

Without another thought, he lifted her into his arms and kicked the door closed. She squeaked her disapproval, but he ignored her and carried her up to the front porch. The overhead light came on, operating under a sensor.

"The key's under the mat," she signed.

Owen gently deposited her back onto her feet to retrieve it and unlock the door. "Don't leave the key here. It's too dangerous," Owen signed, elbowing the door wide at the same time.

"It's a good thing it was here. After I was nearly run over, I wasn't going anywhere near the street to get my keys back tonight." Miriam stepped past him over the threshold.

Owen's stomach dropped at the visual. He stopped her with a hand to her forearm, needing her full attention. The matter was too important. He reached out to the jagged scrape running along her right cheekbone. The blood had dried, and the wound would heal, but Owen couldn't chase away his sense of foreboding that someone was still coming for Miriam. He needed to know why. "Do you know who's involved with the drugs?"

Miriam jerked away with a swift "No." Her pointer and middle fingers pinched closed with her thumb to make the sign for *no*.

Owen raced ahead of her as she made her way through the living room and kitchen. "Listen to me." He was in her face, but he needed to make sure she understood the danger. "These warning signs to leave the island have crossed the line to alarming and dangerous. You could have been killed."

"Well, I wasn't, as you can see." She waved her hands down her body and sidestepped around him and the kitchen island. She washed her hands in the sink, her back to him, effectively tuning him out.

Owen grabbed a stool at the island to wait her out, suddenly wishing he could hear her laugh again. He liked her better when she was smiling at him instead of ignoring him.

I shouldn't like her at all, he admonished himself. But there was just something about her that challenged everything he knew to be true.

Like deaf people didn't laugh.

Before the boat crash, Cole's laughter had echoed through the house, the bubbly baby sound as infectious and pure as Miriam's had been in the car. But after the accident, Owen had believed he would never hear Cole's laughter again. The boy had nothing to laugh about anymore.

Except here, this woman disproved his belief.

Owen raised his gaze and caught Miriam's reflection in the window above the sink. She watched him as she dabbed at the cut on her cheek with a wet paper towel.

Their eyes met in the glass and held in silence. He could tell by her downturned lips that she fumed, but he didn't get the feeling her anger was directed at him. But who, then?

After a few moments, her tense shoulders seemed to relax. She tossed the towel into the trash bin and faced him. "You look sad," she signed.

Her statement caught him off guard. She'd been assessing his lingering skeletons just as he'd been assessing hers. But would she think him crass if he voiced his? Probably, but honesty seemed the best route. "I like you better when you're laughing." He bit down on his back teeth before pushing on with. "But, honestly, I didn't think it was possible for a deaf person to laugh."

Miriam winced. Her stunned expression drove him to explain. "I haven't heard my son laugh since before the accident that left him deaf."

She sighed deeply and placed her hand over her heart. A simple gesture that put him at ease, knowing he hadn't offended her. That he could talk openly with her and she would understand.

Once again, that unexpected feeling of acceptance washed over him.

Owen watched her walk over to the refrigerator. "What's your son's name?" she signed as she opened the fridge.

"C-O-L-E." He signed out the letters.

"What do you call him?" She spoke with one hand as she filled her other with a carton of eggs and butter, then hip-checked the door closed. Her movements flowed in such a natural and comfortable way that Owen wondered how long it had taken her to reach a place in her life where she was okay with her disability.

"C-O-L-E." He re-signed the letters to answer her question.

She planted her supplies on the island across from him and sized him up with quizzical eyes. "No, I mean, what is his name sign? When someone signs to me who knows me, they don't spell out M-I-R-I-A-M. They call me…" Miriam made the sign of the word *swim* using the letter *M* with it. Both her hands, positioned in the letter *M,* paddled out in front of her in two small breaststroke motions. "See? That's what people call me. I began swimming in junior high school. My swim coach was also a sign-language interpreter and gave me the name sign. I've used it ever since. So what is your son's name sign?"

Owen sat speechless; his arms dropped slowly to the cool, yellow top of the island. He hooked the back treads of his hiker boots on the bottom rung of the wooden stool and straightened uncomfortably under her question. It hung between them like the pots and pans above the island, then banged in his head as loudly as the one she took down and dropped on the counter.

Miriam withdrew her attention from him and directed it to her cooking task. Her movements around the kitchen went from comfortable flowing to rigid efficiency. But knowing how she'd handled multiple tasks before, and conversed as she did so, told him her withdrawal from this conversation was deliberate.

Eggs cracked a little harder than necessary. Flour puffed into the air. Walnuts took a beating on the chopping block. Spoons whipped around batter-filled bowls with angry exuberance.

She was angry again, and this time it *was* his fault.

"Miriam," he spoke aloud without thinking. The sound of his voice filled the room and bounced back at him. The echo accentuated the fact that it was the first word from his lips since he'd arrived. His contentedness to sit in silence and speak her language nearly knocked him off the stool.

It seemed signing to her came so much more easily than signing to his son. But then again, Cole was a constant reminder of Owen's transgressions. That was a barrier Owen didn't think he could ever get past. Nor should he. His son would never have a normal life because of him.

Except this woman kept disproving that.

Miriam bent to open her oven and placed the tray of cookies on the rack. She whisked back to the refrigerator and plucked out selections of produce, only to resume with the fierce chopping again.

Approaching her with a knife in her hand might not end well for him, but Owen needed to get her attention. Her silent treatment went beyond withholding words. The way she could literally tune him out meant he might as well not be in the room. Without her attention on him, he could say nothing to fix what he'd done wrong—whatever that was. He still wasn't positive, but he had an idea it had to do with her disappointment in the upbringing of his son. And honestly he would have to agree that he was a horrible father, which was why Cole now lived with Rebecca's parents, where Owen couldn't hurt him anymore.

Owen stood and met Miriam around the island. He placed a hand on her shoulder and felt her stiffen beneath his loose grasp. When he heard the knife drop from her hand with a clatter, he took it as a good sign. Her shoulders stooped inward on a sigh before she turned to face him.

The anger that had pinched up her face had turned to melancholy. Her sad eyes stopped his "sins of the father" confession.

"My mother wouldn't let me sign around her," Miriam signed with slow, deliberate effort. "She said it embarrassed her. She said it made me look like a freak. She said I was the reason my dad didn't stick around. He didn't want me because of my deafness." Miriam lowered her hands to her chest as though it ached. Her gray eyes pooled, and Owen took a step closer. Her hands rose to stop him and to ask the question he didn't want to hear. "Do you not want your son because he is deaf?"

Owen gulped at her question. He shook his head to deny her words, but from where she stood it probably looked that way. How could he tell her the truth, though? And why did it feel so important to him that he did? What was this woman to him? Saying she was nothing didn't feel right. Whether he embraced their connection or not, he had to admit there was one, and maybe, just maybe, he was here on this island for more than a drug investigation.

Owen whipped around to the faucet. He turned his back on her and her question, and Miriam took that as his answer.

He didn't want his son because of his deafness. She bit the inside of her cheek to mask the pain she felt in her heart for that little boy. She knew first-hand how lonely a home could be when there was no one to talk to and no one who wanted to make the effort to learn how.

Except Owen *had* learned sign language. And not just a few signs to get by. He was fluent. Why would he make the effort if he didn't plan to use it to speak with his son?

She pondered that as she picked up her knife to finish the salad. Regardless of her disappointment in his fathering, she had a dinner to make. Miriam had her first guest in her home. He wasn't there for hospitality, but she could still share a nice meal with him.

Owen hadn't mentioned any plans for dinner, but if he really meant what he'd said about not leaving her side, then that would include staying for dinner.

She did need to speak with him about what exactly that would mean for later. As much as she loved having a guest up on her cliff, he couldn't stay. That would not be a good idea or an appropriate situation for a single woman living on her own. First of all, it was against her godly character to put herself in such a situation. Second, even though she couldn't hear the whispers from the islanders, she knew they would fly.

Miriam had made sure Nick had adequate housing before she'd made the move with him for that reason. Even though their relationship was business related, having him there would not be appropriate. She'd found him an available cabin rental down at the pier. It was one of those cute little white clapboard things with a front porch that reminded her of summer camp. Plus, he had the best view overlooking the sea. She could have been very cozy in one of those cabins if she hadn't had a house already.

Owen sidled up, armed with a knife. She ceased her cucumber massacre with a pointed stare. He smirked and grabbed a tomato, and, with that, she guessed he was staying for dinner.

Her blade fell in unison with his as they sliced and diced. Twice his elbow hit hers and she realized he was left-handed. She supposed she could have moved over a bit, but she kind of liked the tingling waves that traveled up her arm when he bumped her, and *he* didn't seem to be in any hurry to move over.

With nothing left to cut, she grabbed the underside of the board to pick it up and scrape the veggies into the bowl with the waiting lettuce. Only, Owen grabbed the board at the same time, and before she could change their course, tomato and cucumber pieces headed in the wrong direction.

Green and red diced veggies flew through the air like confetti at a Christmas fiesta. One by one, each piece landed in too many different places to warrant even an attempt at saving them. There was nothing to do but watch and accept the demise of her salad—and hospitality.

She gave her best grin and signed, "At least we still have the cookies."

Owen's dark eyes flashed with remorse. His hand fisted at his chest to sign, "I'm sorry. I wanted to help, but you were doing fine without me. I should have stayed over there. I should have stayed out of your way."

Out of my way? He wanted to avoid me, like everyone else? "What if I told you I was tired of people staying out of my way?"

His head tilted a bit. "What do you mean?"

"You're my first visitor. When I came here, all I wanted was to make some friends. Instead, I walk down the boardwalk and the people dip back inside or cross so they won't pass me by. If they do pass, they barely look me in the eyes."

"I'm sure they only do these things because of Nick. He's probably been misrepresenting you since you arrived."

"Possibly, but I think they're also uncomfortable around me because of the language barrier. They choose to avoid me instead. They choose to stay out of my way, when all I want is for them to—"

The lights flickered.

Owen's stoic expression seemed to dare her to continue with the truth. "Do you need to get that?"

She nodded but didn't move.

The lights flickered again, snapping her into motion. She left him alone in the kitchen, deciding it was best to not play this truth-and-dare game.

Her phone system sat on her desk in the living room. She pushed the button to answer. A message scrawled across the screen. Look out your front window.

As she pivoted to follow the directions, she collided with Owen's chest. Miriam jumped back and saw his eyes weren't on her but on the screen. He read along, then without a word, made his way to the front parlor in brisk strides.

She followed on his heels to the front bay window. He blocked her view with the height he had on her, but on her tiptoes, she could make out something silhouetted in the moonlight at the end of her pebbled walkway. Owen's arm came back around, shoving her away from the window before she could identify the object.

"Stay!" his hand commanded, then reached behind his waist and removed a gun she'd had no idea he had on him. Stunned by the shiny black weapon, positioned at the ready in his hand, she felt her legs lock in place as he flipped up the safety latch.

He swung the front door wide and peered out from beside the doorjamb. After a tense moment, Owen slunk out onto the front porch with careful steps. From there, he disappeared from view.

Miriam inched forward to investigate what was out there that would make him react with such caution. Owen had told her to stay, but if she was careful not to be seen from the window, then she would be safe. Besides, Owen might need her assistance. To do what, she wasn't sure, but she still figured she should know what was going on in front of her house.

She dropped to a crouch and crawled to eye level with the window trim, then nudged up a little more to get a clear view of the walkway.

Owen's back hunched over the object, blocking her view. His gun protruded from the waistband of his pants, glinting off the porch light. If he'd holstered it, did that mean the coast was clear and it was safe for her to proceed, as well?

With that thought, she gained her feet and went to the front door. She halted at the threshold when she could make out a dark liquid on the white pebbles. A coffee spill came to mind. Perhaps it was her wishful thinking because the truth was too hard to grasp.

If that was blood on her walkway, then the object was a living thing. And it was hurt.

An animal? A person? She turned away, toward the direction of her phone. She could call the TTY operator and have them call 911. But what would she tell them? At this point, she didn't know what was out there.

She veered back. Owen had a phone to his ear, already making the call. That eased her from feeling like a failure in the situation. She wanted to help, but it would take her longer to be productive if she had to use her phone service. His lips were moving, but in the dark shadows and with only a view of his profile, she couldn't make out his words.

She wished he would move so she could see behind him. She craned her neck to try, then realized she was on the bottom stair. She'd left the house without making the conscious decision, as though her legs had a mind of their own.

He straightened and pocketed his phone. On her first step down on the pebbles, he sprang around to face her. He must have heard her. His lips moved fast and demanding and completely soundless. She tore her gaze from his useless words and dropped it to the clear view she now had of the object behind him.

Nick lay curled up, unconscious and bloodied at the end of her walkway.

SEVEN

Someone had beaten up Nick. Miriam's hands twisted together in her lap. Someone had beaten him within an inch of his life and left him on her front curb like yesterday's garbage. Someone had used him to get to her all because they wanted her to leave the island and had grown tired of asking.

She'd thought the pranks were coming from a student and had figured eventually the identity of the troublemaker would come to light. As principal, she would handle it internally. But this attack went beyond juvenile shenanigans. Nick was a grown man, even if he was on the smaller side. Miriam could no longer discount the local adults as possible suspects in the pranks and in Nick's assault.

She should have listened to Nick when he'd told her to call the police. She should have notified Sherriff Grant after the first onslaught. As soon as the first message came, she should have filed a report. Now Nick lay on one of the only two clinic beds on the island, coughing up the price of her stubbornness as he'd been coughing up blood on her walkway.

Dr. Schaffer pulled the chair up in front of her. He spoke slowly and loudly to her. Under other circumstances she might have smiled at his unconscious attempt to make her hear him, but right now her lips were pursed so tight, bending them into a smile would require the mending of her shame-filled heart.

Nick was hurt because of her.

Miriam turned away from the lip-flapping doctor to face Owen in the seat across from her. "Can you please tell him I can't understand him?"

No trace of comprehension crossed his face. His undercover signing secret remained intact.

"He's a doctor," she signed, not caring about his secret at the moment. "Everything is confidential, isn't it?"

Owen turned his attention to the glass doors, where the lit walkway led to a quiet downtown.

So that's it? She fumed. She was on her own? Her interpreter, the only person on this island who could translate for her, lay sedated, leaving her less valuable than a planter in the corner of the room, and now the high-and-mighty special agent chose to abandon her to flounder alone. Fury seeped out of Miriam like steam off hot pavement.

She hated that she had this anger deep down inside her. It wasn't as though she was the first child to go through life without her parents' blessing of acceptance. She supposed that was why she could always relate to Esau's story in the Book of Genesis. When Esau's father gave his blessing to his brother and not to him, Miriam felt Esau's anguish as if it was her own. When he cried out, "Bless me, even me also, O my father!" she cried out the same thing.

Even me.

How she'd craved her mother's acceptance. Her blessing. Instead Miriam had been left in the darkness, empty-handed.

Until God met her there and gave her His perfect blessing.

Miriam closed her eyes, ignoring the doctor's soundless words, ignoring Owen's undercover stand. Ignoring the world she didn't belong in and calling on the one she did. She sighed and leaned her head back against the wall.

I feel alone, Father, she prayed silently. *I don't know who to trust anymore, and I don't know why You brought me here. I need Your healing and guiding hand. Please, Father, remove the haze of my anger so I can see Your ways clearly. So I can hear Your direction for my life. So I can receive the blessings You have for me.*

Something touched her arm. Miriam opened her eyes to find Owen had moved across the room to the chair beside her. Worry etched his features.

"Are you okay?" he signed, and she noticed the doctor had left the room.

"I'm fine. I was talking to God."

His eyes flashed in surprise, then dulled to annoyance. "Excuse me if I don't join you. God left me when I needed Him most. And from where I stand, it doesn't look like He's doing much for you, either."

Owen was wrong. He didn't know God the way she did. He wasn't there in the darkness with her. No one was. No one but God. She could always trust Him to lead her out.

"Dr. Schaffer says Nick will be okay. He should be able to leave in a couple days. We can stay by his side tonight if you want," Owen said.

"Shouldn't Nick be transported to the mainland?" Miriam asked. Dr. Shaffer was a good physician, but a hospital would be best.

"No," Owen answered. "There are no signs of internal bleeding. The blood came from the stomach, not the lungs. Judging by the bruise in the shape of a boot, it was caused by a kick to the abdomen."

"Kicked? As in stomped on when he was down? After they had already battered his face and roughed him up, they finished him off with a blow that could have killed him?" Miriam breathed deeply; the smell of antiseptic and everything sterile filled her nostrils. She let herself grow used to the sharp clinical smells, a reminder that Nick was in the right place. God had provided, and Nick would heal.

Her quick-to-anger response chagrined her. Lately she'd been falling off the edge of anger a little too often for her liking. This was the third time today. First this morning when she'd thought Owen had judged Ben stereotypically, and then at her house when Owen didn't deny how he treated his son. Slow to anger had always been her prayer of petition, but at the moment she didn't feel like giving it up.

She justified the lapse, saying an innocent person had been hurt, even though deep down she knew her anger wouldn't help anyone heal—or receive justice.

Through the double glass doors, Miriam noticed a woman rushing up the concrete walk. Before the doors were flung wide, she recognized the woman as her secretary.

Stephanie burst in, her hands and mouth moving a frantic mile a minute. Miriam sprang up and signed to Owen, "What is she saying?"

He gave a single shake of his head.

"Please, I need to know what's made her so upset."

Owen eluded her request with a blank face.

Slow to anger, Miriam prayed, needing peace more than ever when it came to this man.

She targeted her secretary's lips. Miriam recognized Nick's name—and the longing look of affection Stephanie sent toward his room.

Miriam did a double take. It couldn't be true, she thought. *Could it?*

Stephanie was a bangle-clinking fiasco. The way her arms flew around with each of her wails, Owen thought she might knock someone out with those bracelets, especially the jewel-encrusted ones. "I can't believe this has happened," she droned on. "Where is he? I need to make sure he's okay."

"Are you talking about Nick?" Owen speculated on how this girl had learned about the assault already. And what was Nick to her anyway?

"Yes! Where is he? Is it bad?" She bounced on her tiptoes in an attempt to peer beyond him.

"Well, it's not good, but he'll be fine. Someone did a number on him. You wouldn't happen to know who that someone is, would you?"

Stephanie landed back on her feet, her eyes an act of wide-eyed innocence. "Me? No, how would I know?"

"Well, you found out he was here. How did you know he was hurt?"

"Well, Tildy told me, of course." She seemed surprised that he didn't know this already.

"Who's Tildy?"

"Tildy. You know. Tildy from the Underground Küchen."

"What is the Underground Küchen?"

She flipped her wrist with a jingle. "Oh, yeah, I forgot. You've only been here for a couple days. It's the German restaurant, down by the shore. The one carved into the cliff."

"Right." Nick had mentioned the place to him. "And how did Tildy find out about Nick?"

"Ah, let me see." Stephanie rolled her eyes to the ceiling. Owen suspected this could take a while. Steph wasn't proving to be as bright as the pink concoction she wore for a blouse. "Tildy told me that Len told her."

"Len? The custodian?"

"Yes. She said Len stopped in for his usual and told her that Frank had heard that Nick was here."

"Frank?" Owen recalled Wes mentioning a Frank before.

"Frank Thibodaux."

"Thibodaux." The name clicked. "Any relation to Ben?"

"His grandfather. The two men own the two restaurants on the island."

"They have a vested interest in this island, then. And if someone doesn't fit in, they might even take matters into their own hands to get rid of them."

"Well, that seems kind of harsh." Stephanie jutted out her chin. "Hey, are you saying Frank and Len beat up Nick? Don't you know how ridiculous that sounds? They're like ninety years old or something. Plus, they are sweet old men who love us all." Stephanie nodded at Miriam. "In fact, they were the ones who hired her in the first place."

"Wait, it was Frank and Len who made the decision to hire Ms. Hunter?"

"Yes. They said it was time to bring her home. Now, can I please see Nick?"

* * *

"I had no idea Stephanie felt this way about Nick," Miriam signed to Owen in the waiting room. "She kept her feelings a secret from me, and apparently Nick, too."

Miriam hoped from Nick, too. With him sedated she couldn't ask him outright. She almost dreaded the moment he would awake. Would this be another thing he'd kept from her?

"How well do you know Frank Thibodaux and Len Smith?" Owen asked.

"Apparently as well as I know Nick." She waved her hands to indicate he could ignore that last off-the-cuff statement. "They seem like very nice men, but I don't know them well. Why?"

"Did you know it was their decision to hire you?"

Her curiosity was piqued. "They sit on the school board. In fact, now that I think about it, I think they sit on every board. They must be revered by the islanders."

"Yes, seemingly so. But why would they hire you?"

Miriam scoffed at his insult. "Because I qualified for the job and earned my way here."

"I'm sorry, but you have to see it is highly unusual for a deaf person to be in charge of a hearing school, no matter how qualified you are for the job."

The guy might as well have pushed her off her cliff. Did he really believe what he was saying?

"Criminal behavior is happening on this island." He continued to sign as though he hadn't just cut her down. "Somehow you're connected. I need to figure out how. So tell me, how did you hear about the job?"

She pursed her lips and looked away, not wanting to tell him anything. But then she figured he thought that way about her only because he didn't know her well enough yet. She just had to show him how smart she was. Her swim coach always told her she had to get out there and show the world how smart she was, and that would include Owen.

"I received a letter from the school board soon after the reading of the will. I inherited the house but wasn't planning on returning here. I thought I would just sell it," Miriam signed, thinking back. "Then I got the letter. I remember it came with a picture of my grandparents and said it would make them proud to have their only grandchild living in their home and a part of Stepping Stones. They offered me a position I had been waiting for—to head my own school. But I'll admit the 'a part of' in the letter was what had me making plans to accept." She tilted her head in thought. "Do you think they knew what to say to get me to come back?"

"They definitely played on your emotions."

"But why? And who's against it to the point they would beat Nick up to make me leave?"

"Who was the principal before you? Why did

they leave?" Owen leaned in, his eyes sharpened to points. She could practically see the gears in his mind cranking.

Miriam felt grateful for his presence and his help. Without Owen, she would be sitting here, scared out of her mind without a clue to what was going on. Someone out there didn't know Owen could sign and probably thought without her interpreter, she would be on the first helicopter off the island. Whoever it was probably figured she wouldn't even wait for the Sunday ferry that came in two days.

She signed, "I was told the man before me retired to Florida. He was part of the Thibodaux family."

Owen chewed on that for a few moments before speaking again. "The Thibodaux family seems to be gaining high-alert status in this investigation. Perhaps they're involved in more than committee boards. Perhaps drug smuggling is their next business venture."

"But what does it have to do with me?"

"I'm not sure yet. I think tomorrow I'll be in the mood for some German food, though."

EIGHT

Saturday lunch at the Underground Küchen bustled with boisterous camaraderie. Trying to find a table or a spot at the bar proved useless, and when a lively little ditty broke out, Owen got caught in a human wave that eventually delivered him to the back corner by the kitchen—or *küchen,* as they said in German.

He missed the swinging door coming at him by mere inches and came face-to-face with a middle-aged waitress squeezed into a green velour bodice laced up over white frills.

"Oops, didn't see you there." The woman lingered for a beat while she slanted her coiffed head in his direction. "Hey, aren't you the new teacher?"

"Yes, I'm Owen Matthews, the new English teacher. I heard great things about this place, but I had no idea it would be this crazy. Is it always like this?"

She cackled and pushed a pen into her shellacked, bleached hair. "Only at certain hours of the day. I'm

Tildy. It's nice to meet you. Come, I'll set you up by the bar. Can't have you sitting by the kitchen for your first visit."

She led the way, parting the sea of people with a wave of her manicured hand. Behind the bar, she pulled out a stool. "Sit. We serve meat here. If you're looking for seafood, then you've come to the wrong place. That fishy stuff is at the other restaurant at the other end of the boardwalk."

Owen sensed a rivalry between the two restaurants, and as much as his interest was piqued, going with the flow of this place would be his best course of action if he was going to get his questions answered. "I'll take the special," he hollered over the din.

The crowd fell silent. First the people nearest him, then whispers went out until they reached every ear. A fork clattered. Someone scoffed loudly.

"Well, you heard what he said," Tildy announced, a smile growing so wide it popped out her laugh lines. "Give the man the special!"

A bell clanged at the other end of the bar.

Not a good sign, in Owen's estimation.

Another frilly waitress bounced off to the kitchen. She returned moments later, backing out of the swinging door because her hands and arms were laden with multiple dishes. He denied they were all for him even though she headed in his direction.

"Are you a praying man, Mr. Matthews?" Tildy

asked as the first platter thumped down in front of him. The plumpest, juiciest knockwurst encircled the rim twice. Curved like a huge pair of smiling lips, it looked like his food laughed at him.

He shook his head at the daunting sight. "Not anymore," he mumbled.

"Well, you might want to get right with God before you dig in. You're going to need Him more than ever before." She cackled as she filled a large stein and sloshed it down in front of him. *"Feierabend!"* she yelled.

"Feierabend!" voices echoed in unison, then started up another rowdy song. Owen believed it was an old Irish melody and not German at all, but who was he to ruin their fun?

He peeled his eyes from his heaping plates and lifted his gaze to the jovial group. Genuine smiles encouraged him to dig in. Bright eyes seemed eager to bask in his victory. He thought that was interesting. They wanted him to succeed, not fail.

With a knife and fork in his hands, he mumbled, *"Feierabend,"* whatever that meant, and sliced his first piece. The pop of the tight knockwurst skin could be heard on the other side of the room, and the crowd roared.

The man nearest him slapped his back. "Do you need some help with any of this? I'd be glad to lighten your load, unless of course you have a death wish."

A death wish.

The words slammed into him. So many times he'd actually wished for exactly that. Wishing it could have been him instead of Rebecca. Wishing one of the dangerous jobs he took on would finally dole out his correct punishment.

Death.

That's what he deserved, and yet here he still sat, alive and well. Instead his innocent wife had paid the price, and his son, who never hurt a living soul, continued to pay daily.

It hit Owen that he hadn't thought about Rebecca's death in a couple days.

The knockwurst in his mouth soured. His stomach revolted as he pushed the bite down.

He frantically attempted to pull an image of his wife from the recesses of his brain, but instead another woman appeared behind his eyelids. A certain redhead gazed back at him with something blazing in her gray eyes.

Forgiveness.

He pushed his plate away and stood up. His hands slipped against the bar's rail. They were drenched in a cold sweat. A vicious scrub to his eyes did nothing to remove her image. He didn't want her there, and he didn't want what she was offering. She was nothing to him but a job. And she sure wasn't the person to be offering him forgiveness.

"Are you okay, man? I was just joking. This stuff

won't really kill you. I've been eating it all my fifty years. A horse has got nothing on my health." The man pounded his chest. Owen zeroed in on a gold ring the man wore. The letter *T,* affixed in black, glinted back at him. He impressed the image into his brain to replace the one of Miriam.

Breathing deeply, Owen reseated himself on his stool. A few people around him observed him with concerned expressions. "Sorry," he said. "Something didn't go down right." He feigned a smile at their nods and picked up his fork. *"Feierabend,"* he said. It was halfhearted but enough to lighten the mood again.

"Feierabend!" someone yelled, and the song restarted. All attention was effectively diverted off him.

"I'm Jerome, by the way." The man next to him put out his hand to shake. "Jerome Thibodaux."

Ah, the infamous Thibodaux family. An opportunity to do some digging had presented itself. "I have a Ben Thibodaux in one of my classes. Any relation?"

"My son." A few strings of sauerkraut hung from the corners of Jerome's full mouth.

"He's a good kid. Smart." Owen sliced a piece of the knockwurst.

"Well, that's the first time someone's ever said that about him. Are you sure we're talking about the same kid?"

"I think so. Wears a lot of black."

"Yup, that's him all right." Jerome shook his head. "After his mother left, I did the best I could raising him, but somewhere along the way I lost him."

Owen soaked up the information. Without a file to read up on Ben's life, Owen would take every morsel of info he could get his hands on. "Sorry, to hear that. Divorce is never easy on anyone, especially the kids."

"Oh, Ben doesn't remember his mother. He was a baby when Rita left. She didn't want to live on the island anymore. Thought it was too isolated. And poof!" Jerome snapped his thick, stubby fingers. "She took off with nothing but a Dear John letter in her wake."

"So you were left to raise your son alone? Do you have any other kids?"

"Nah, just me and Ben. How about you? Do you have any kids?"

"Yes. A son, too. He's eight."

"What's his name?"

Owen started to say Cole, but an image popped into his mind, halting him. The image of a cameraman cranking the camera. Owen chuckled out loud. "His name is Cole. He loves anything to do with pictures, especially video."

"Cool." Jerome speared a potato and shoved it into his mouth whole. "Mmm-mmm-mmm. Tildy is amazing. I always knew I picked the wrong woman."

He nodded at the plate in front of Owen. "Dig in before it gets cold."

Owen took another bite. "So what do you do for a living?"

"Just another lobster boat captain. Makes for long, lonely days out to sea and back. Not much to do out there but pick up my pot."

Owen cut him a glance. "Did you just say *pot?*"

Jerome's roar of laughter turned to a fit of coughing. "I like you, Owen." Jerome shook a speared potato at him. "No, I said pots, as in lobster pots, traps, you know. You just misunderstood with all the noise in here."

Owen agreed with a nod, but he speculated. Why *couldn't* the pot be of the marijuana variety? The lobster boat could be a cover.

The swinging door to the kitchen swung wide. Len Smith's old frame ambled through the door, and people hollered a greeting and made way for him. He acknowledged them all with a single wave and took the offered seat on the other side of Owen.

"Hello there, son." Len stretched his neck to look down the bar. He gave a nod to the waitress. "The usual."

"Mr. Smith," Owen greeted the man. "How do you do?"

"I could ask the same of you. Any luck on figuring out that mishap with the school's electrical panel?"

"Not yet, but I'm working on it."

"Good. There seems to be quite the multitude of accidents occurring lately. Don't get scared off just yet. Stepping Stones really is a pleasant place to live."

Owen gestured to the crowd around them. "It seems like it. I've been given a pretty warm welcome here."

"Glad to hear it."

"So do you work in the kitchen, too?" Owen referenced the swinging door the old man had come through.

"No, I used the back door."

"Back door? This place is built into a cliff. How could there be a back door?"

Len chuckled. "It's a stairway passage, leading up to the top of the cliff. My house is perched right above us, overlooking the sea. Let's just say I have my own direct route to the ocean, and this lovely establishment."

"So you don't have to take the road down. That's convenient," Owen stated.

"Yes, it is. Wouldn't you agree my passageway is convenient, Jerome?" Len leaned forward for a pointed stare across Owen.

With his mouth full of food, Jerome answered, "Very."

Len waved the waitress on. "I'm going to grab my

lunch in the kitchen and take it to go. Enjoy your meal, son." He stood from his stool.

"Please wait." Owen stopped him.

"Yes? You need something?"

"I was curious how you came by the knowledge of Nick Danforth's assault yesterday. The school secretary said she heard the news from Tildy, who heard it from you."

"Oh, well, it's a small town, but I believe it was Frank who told me."

"Frank Thibodaux?" Owen eyed Jerome. "Your father?"

Jerome nodded.

"And how do I find him?"

"Well, you won't find him here, that's for sure. He wouldn't step foot in this place." Jerome guffawed, an unpleasant sight with his mouthful of food.

Owen winced. "Why's that?"

"He owns the restaurant at the other end of the pier."

The rivalry. Owen made a mental note to skip the special at his next stop. "Thank you, sir." He nodded to Len for his help and let the man get his lunch through the swinging doors.

Owen reclined to get a quick glimpse inside. A look around that passageway felt like a must. Was it lit? Did everyone know about it? He would talk to Wes first thing to see about getting access to it.

Owen missed the waitress carrying a tray of desserts to him. The German delights caused his throat to close in revolt. "Please tell me those are not all for me."

"They sure are! Eat up, big guy! *Feierabend!*" she yelled and re-riled the crowd. But before a song could break out in full tilt, the voices died out as quickly as they'd revved up. Owen scanned the room for the cause in the atmospheric drop.

A shadowed figure stood by the door, backlit by sunlight.

Apparently an unwelcome visitor. Cold tension chilled the air. The person stepped out of the shadow, and Owen's heart stuttered for a few beats.

Miriam stood at the end of the bar.

The sick emotion ctched on her face had Owen pushing his plate away. She raised her hands and signed, "When you didn't come back to the clinic, I got worried. But I can see you're doing fine. Better than I've done in seven months."

She turned and walked out. Awkward silence filled the long narrow room.

"Do you know what she said?" Tildy sliced into the uneasiness.

Owen shook his head, regretting what he had to say. "I have no idea."

She clucked her tongue and swatted her towel on the edge of the bar. "And that there lies the problem, doesn't it? She doesn't understand us, and we don't understand her. A real shame, it is."

Owen withdrew his wallet and tossed a few bills on the counter. Concern for Miriam's safety propelled him toward the door. She shouldn't be walking around alone. Someone wanted her off the island, and judging by the subdued and chilly atmosphere left behind in the Underground Küchen, it could be any one of these people.

Miriam craved the one place where she felt free. The one place she felt at home. And it wasn't her house.

Even with its few happy memories to draw on, something about her house wouldn't let her breathe deeply. Deep breathing came only when she was in the water.

After trekking along the shoreline and up her sandy pathway to the cliff-top house for her swimsuit, Miriam returned to slice the frigid water with a dive.

Fall had closed in, dropping water temps. Each swim, she came to grips with the fact that it might be her last of the season. Today was no different. The cold froze her toes so quickly she nearly stuck close to shore instead of taking her usual course to the stones.

Swimming in the waves required thoughtful planning. Miriam needed to know her tidal times and be aware of the undertow that could take her. She needed to make smart decisions out here. One slipup could mean a watery grave.

A pause in her strokes every few minutes kept her on course. At one check, she swirled around in a circle as waves gently lifted and dropped her. The flavor of salt touched her lips with each undulation.

Her typical destination of the lighthouse was out. A certain someone would invade her mind if she went there today. It would have to be a different rock. One that didn't have a memory attached to it. She only hoped she would be able to climb up safely. Some stones didn't allow for easy access with their straight, slick height.

She scanned the horizon, spotting a low rock about fifty yards past the lighthouse. It would require more of a swim, but it was still safe and doable.

Miriam moved into a breaststroke, cutting the water with her smooth form and rhythm. The rock popped in and out of her view with each lift of her head from the icy water. Her extremities were losing feeling. Swimming this far out might have been a poor decision.

Ahead, water sloshed against the gray stone, leaving white foam behind. She pushed through with another stroke and stopped for another survey of her proximity. About twenty-five yards left. She swirled in a circle to check her distance from the shoreline and jolted in alarm.

A fisherman's boat barreled down on her. The driver must not see her in his path, she figured. She threw her arm high and waved wide and rapidly, praying they would see her.

The boat stayed the course straight toward her.

Panic spiraled up her throat and choked her. Miriam fumbled back and pushed at the water, her arms like flapping paddles. A fruitless technique, but it seemed her knowledge of accurate swim strokes had fled from her mind.

Water sloshed over her. Freezing gulps of it filled her mouth, pushing her down. She couldn't be going under. *She couldn't.* She was an expert swimmer. Water burned her eyes. Her head felt the pressure of the water's weight above her. She'd submerged.

Miriam pushed to resurface, breaking free for the moment. It didn't matter that she was an expert swimmer. She knew the signs of a drowning victim, and right now, in her panicked state, she was in aquatic distress. With each mouthful of water and absence of air to her lungs, her splashes would begin to slow to nothing. From there, instinctive drowning response would set in. Once that happened, the sea would swallow her in less than twenty seconds...*if* the boat didn't hit her first.

She needed to force her body to react with the precise stroke that would move her. The backstroke would take her from the boat's path. Her brain knew that, but the message failed to reach her limbs. *Backstroke,* she restated, triggering her body to engage.

She spit the water out and sent her arm flying back. The stroke pulled her up and out of the water, back at least five feet. Air filled her lungs to capacity and gave her enough strength to swing back the other arm, then the other, again and again.

The boat's bow remained on her, pointing the way to disaster. Was he *trying* to aim for her like the truck had? There would be no trees to escape to out here.

Miriam pushed for another rotation of strokes, the waves thwarting her efforts. Her breathing came short and was interrupted with swigs of brackish seawater.

She couldn't give up. Her arms worked another set, bringing her closer to the rock. *Move, move,* she rammed home in her mind with every stroke, even as she could see the boat tracking her. There was no way to outswim it. Miriam accepted the collision even as she heaved through one more rotation.

The hull of the boat towered over her. It was so formidable in its speeding approach, she stopped breathing at the sight. It would sink her in less than a second. Miriam kicked hard, praying she could skirt the hull. Water gushed at her like a plow, sinking her down. She grasped at nothing; the boat's wake was powerful enough to hold her below the surface.

And yet she hadn't been hit.

Miriam felt the boat fly by her. Had the bow changed its course and veered away? She swung her arm back for another backstroke to pull away farther while she still could, but her hand smacked into something hard.

The rock. She'd made it to the rock.

And if the boat hadn't changed course it would have hit the rock, too.

Miriam's hands bit into sharp barnacles as she clung to the rock for dear life. She had to get to safety, and this rock wasn't it. What if they came back? Her position wouldn't stop them from harming her. If anything, she'd made herself an easy target. Especially since nobody knew she went swimming. She ignored the fact that even if they did know, she didn't think anyone would come for her.

Owen circled the outside of Miriam's house. Her Vespa sat parked in the driveway. The same place he'd moved it to last night after the ambulance had transported Nick. Owen's chest heaved from running up the narrow, sandy path from her shoreline. He thought maybe she'd gone for a swim out to the lighthouse, but when he'd scanned the rock from shore, it appeared vacant.

His first stop had been the clinic, where an awakened Nick had said he hadn't seen her since she'd left to go find him.

I shouldn't have left her alone in the first place.
Owen slammed a fist into his thigh.

"Is Ms. Hunter here?" A voice came from behind him.

Owen whipped around to find Wes and one of his deputies. "Hey, Wes. Actually, I'm looking for her, too. What do you need?"

"The warrant I've been waiting for came in." He slapped a tri-folded slip of paper against his palm.

"Warrant? I haven't seen any evidence against Miriam to make a warrant necessary. If anything, after the theft and burning of her car and Nick's assault, they should be exonerated. Protected even."

"Well, then, a quick search won't hurt anybody." Wes took the back steps and opened the screen door.

"Wes, I think you should wait until she's home." Owen pleaded from the bottom step. A sick feeling settled in the pit of his stomach. "Please, Wes. This is really going to hurt her. It might even send her packing."

The sheriff turned around with his back to the door. "It would seem you've let your personal feelings get in the way of the job, *Agent* Matthews. If you don't remember, Owen, we went to the same police academy, and as I recall, that's a no-no." With that he jabbed an elbow back and broke the small square pane of glass closest to the doorknob.

Glass tinkling to Miriam's kitchen floor filtered to Owen's ears as he set off to find her in earnest.

* * *

Owen checked the boat lights for the third time. With dusk settling, he couldn't be caught out on the water in the dark. If his lights didn't work he'd have no way to illuminate his course—and no way for another boat to see him.

The fact that he found himself back in a boat, the one place he didn't belong, made him wonder if Wes has been right.

Maybe he had lost his focus.

Because of a certain little redhead.

Owen scanned the water's surface for that redhead now.

Short of knocking on strangers' doors, he'd checked every storefront, park bench and doghouse to find her. He'd even peeked into the Underground Küchen again. The rival restaurant had closed early for the day. No explanation was provided at the Blue Lobster.

With the sun dropping behind the island, he didn't have to contend with blinding light in his eyes. Owen's view shot clear to the rocks. The lack of movement on them suggested this was another wild-goose chase.

Owen idled up close to the first rock protruding high out of the water. Too high to scale. He considered the others nearby. One seemed accessible.

He motioned forward, shifting his gaze in all directions for any surprise stones in his path. A collision would be the equivalent to reliving a nightmare.

He scanned the darkening horizon and caught movement. A large bird of some kind? Owen squinted.

Something black flew over the farthest rock. Some kind of bicycle with glider wings, he thought, but it was too far to be sure. Owen kept it in his sight and changed his course, but that meant turning away from the low stone. He gave it a quick glance for movement.

Nothing.

He searched the sky in time to see the flying contraption drop a bundle onto the rock, then cut a wide path back from where it came.

Owen pulled up the throttle, knowing exactly what he'd witnessed.

The drop.

He'd unintentionally ventured into the path of the illegal drug operation.

Owen's senses shot to high alert. The waiting pickup party wouldn't be far. Would they appear if they saw him or hold back?

Or would they just shoot him out of the water?

He turned the boat back to the low rock. The stone's width would shield him while he called for backup. Adrenaline pumped though his veins. This would be the proof Wes needed to pardon Miriam from any wrongdoing. Owen would give Wes the criminal on a silver platter—*if* he stayed alive to catch the guy.

Owen chugged around the rock, dropping anchor when the rock covered him completely. He moved back to the port quarter to pull the rear of his boat closer in. His gaze caught on a familiar mishmash of blue and red in the water. It floated between the boat and rock, and it reminded him of Miriam's swimsuit.

Miriam.

At first his feet stayed locked in place, unable to make a move, then he kicked his body into high gear. Over the port bow, he bent over the side to reach her.

She was on her back. Her eyes were closed, long lashes resting on white skin. Her lips were blue.

He reached down, and stopped right before he touched her. Old, drilled rescue instructions reared their heads. *Don't move a victim. There could be a spinal injury.*

But she needs to get out of the freezing water. "Miriam!" he called uselessly.

Owen pulled his hand back in a fist, slamming it on the boat's rim in frustration. He needed to figure out the safest way to get her out.

He judged the rock. It was low enough that he might be able to slide her up onto it without moving her neck. Standing up on the boat's edge, he stepped over her and secured his footing on the rock. Crouching down, he cupped the back of her head while placing a hand under her armpit.

Her eyes fluttered and closed again. He brought his face within inches. She was upside down to him. He needed to ask her if she was hurt, but he couldn't sign at the moment.

Her lashes fluttered wide. He noticed the typical vibrancy of her eyes had been replaced by a glassy haze. Even if she didn't have anything broken, hypothermia had settled in.

"Miriam, are you hurt?" He spoke clearly, hoping she could read his lips upside down.

Leaving one hand supporting her neck, he withdrew his other hand and used it to half sign, hoping she got the gist. "I need to get you out of the water. I'm going to pull you up."

Her lids fell closed but quickly opened again with a small nod.

Owen breathed a sigh of relief. She was coherent. He reached back under her armpit and hefted her out swiftly. She lay sprawled on the rock, not a muscle shaking. Not a good sign.

Owen jumped back onto his boat for the blanket he'd used the first day he'd met her. He'd covered her that day with the wool blanket, but his thoughts had only been on Rebecca. The memory of losing his wife had pushed him to reach out to help the unknown woman that day.

The idea of losing Miriam propelled him now. As he covered her, a riot of emotions welled up inside, warring against his self-imposed punishment of a lifetime of solitude. He didn't understand them and wanted to deny their existence.

Miriam's glassy eyes gazed up at him. Her hands attempted to move beneath the blanket. "Shhh." He tried to calm her, inches from her face. Her blue lips trembled. He leaned closer to blow his warm breath on them.

She pushed up; her forehead pressed into his. She could move on her own.

Relief swept through him. His eyes closed on an exhale. Again he questioned the emotions careening through him. He nearly thanked God, but he opened his eyes before he did.

Owen noticed he'd drifted closer to Miriam's lips. His eyes locked on them, unable to withdraw from their pull.

Until they shivered again.

He needed to get her warm. The sun had set and the rock offered little remaining heat from the day. They needed to get to the boat or they'd be traveling back in darkness. Owen didn't trust himself to man the boat at night. He needed to keep her alive, not put her in more danger.

Her mouth formed a circle. A sound squeaked from her lips. He struggled to understand what she tried to tell him.

"We'll talk when you're warmed up," he signed. "I'm going to lift you and put you in the boat."

In one swoop, Miriam rested cradled in his arms,

the blanket covering her from chin to toes. Her head nestled into the crook of his arm. A lulling feeling washed over him, which seemed illogical, since he was the one cradling her.

Unless saving Miriam offered him a sense of atonement.

Owen stepped into the port bow, shaking his head at the ludicrous idea. A life for a life was the only way to retribution.

She made the squeaking circle with her shaking lips again. He laid her down on the long cushioned seats in the stern and signed, "Hang on. I'm going to get you to the clinic."

Owen took the controls and pulled up anchor. The rock that contained the dropped package tempted him. More than anything he wanted to retrieve it. The drugs were the real reason he was there, and he had a job to do.

The shivering woman behind him changed all that.

Owen started the engine and called Wes on his cell.

The sheriff answered on the second ring. "Where are you?" he demanded.

Owen zipped forward and set his course for shore. "Wes, get to the pier. The farthest rock to the left has a package on it. Willing to bet it's your drugs. I watched a flying contraption make the drop. But listen, I can't get to it right now."

"Why not?"

Owen hesitated in telling Wes where he'd found Miriam. If Wes knew she was near the drop he would think the worst of her. He would think she was guilty.

"Miriam's ill. I need to get her to the clinic." *And protect her pure heart.*

"That's where you're heading?"

"Roger."

"Okay, I'll see you there."

Owen pocketed his phone and cast a glance at Miriam. She watched him from her prostrate position. So serious were her eyes that his spine shuddered. He recognized gratitude in them, but that wasn't all. Even he couldn't deny the intense closeness growing between them.

Then common sense struck back into him like a lightning bolt of conviction.

Owen whipped forward, breaking their bond before he could destroy another pure heart.

Miriam nestled back into the crook of Owen's arm as he headed straight for the clinic. Never before in all her life had she felt so protected. Not even when she'd dated Andy the lifeguard had she felt looked after and cared for like this.

Nick always joked about her weakness for rescuers, and usually she went along with it for fun, but maybe he was onto something, because in this moment, Owen Matthews was her hero.

She'd lost all feeling in her body and hadn't known how much longer she could perform the standard survival float on her back when he'd shown up out of nowhere. The rock had given her a handle to hold, but with her extremities frozen, she couldn't be completely positive she still grabbed it. Any more time in those frigid waters would have meant death.

Judging by Owen's quick and knowledgeable response, he knew that, too.

She wished she could tell him thank-you, but she couldn't speak with her arms beneath the blanket, and in her frozen state, her mind seemed to inhibit her from forming words on her lips. On the boat, she'd tried to tell him someone had nearly killed her, but by the look of confusion on his face, she'd known her words hadn't been formed correctly.

Owen spun her around at the clinic doors so he could back in. Yesterday, the two of them had brought Nick here. Now it was her turn.

She needed to tell Owen someone had tried to hit her with their boat. That she'd been afraid to get on the rock in case they came back. And swimming back was out of the question.

A nurse appeared, concern on her face. Owen spoke; then she waved them into Nick's room.

Nick's empty room.

Miriam pushed up in Owen's arms, frantically

searching the room for Nick. Where was he? She focused on the nurse's lips and caught, "Nick checked out...." The rest of the words were spoken too quickly to comprehend.

Owen laid her down on the bed. "I'll be right outside. The nurse is going to get you warmed up."

Miriam threw off the blanket to sign, "Where's Nick?"

"The nurse said he had an appointment that he couldn't miss and checked himself out."

She signed quickly before he turned away and left the room. "It's not safe for him out there. Someone tried to kill me."

Owen's eyes pierced her. "What do you mean? How?"

She told him everything, including how grateful she was to him for coming for her.

"You shouldn't be thanking me." Owen's signs jerked sharply as the cords in his neck tensed. "If I hadn't left your side, you'd be fine."

"I'm a big girl and can own up to my own behaviors. You told me not to leave the clinic, and I did. My fault. Not yours."

Owen tapped his chest. "The pain in here tells me I let you down. Not the other way around. I shouldn't have forgotten that you're disabled."

Miriam's breath hitched, unsure if the word *disabled* had really formed on Owen's hands. Had she read that correctly? Maybe he got his signs mixed up. That had to be it. He couldn't really see her as disabled.

Her hands felt cold and stiff as she signed, "You said D-I-S-A-B-L-E-D. Did you mean to say something else?'

"No."

Sheriff Grant stepped into the room before Miriam could reply. The two men exchanged some words, but the rolling anger Miriam could feel rising in her wouldn't allow her to focus on their conversation. All she could think about were the few choice words she had for Owen. One in particular was that she was *not* disabled.

"Sheriff Grant has asked me to translate for him," Owen signed through the growing red haze of her eyes. "I promise I'll tell you exactly what he says and translate your words accurately. Are you okay with me interpreting for you?"

Miriam fisted her hands to refrain from saying what was really on the tips of her fingers. As soon as Sheriff Grant left the room, she would be giving Owen an eyeful. Miriam breathed deeply and signed stiffly, "Sure, go ahead."

Sheriff Grant reached to his belt and removed silver handcuffs. In the next second he had her left hand incased in one cuff. In confusion, she watched him secure the other cuff to the metal railing.

Miriam tugged. The edges of the contraption cut into her skin with each shake and pull. *What is this about?* She sat stupefied. Her gaze traveled from the cuffs to the two men.

Sheriff Grant's lips moved without an ounce of expression on his face.

Owen's expression turned ashen. His chest expanded with a deep breath before he raised his arms and translated the sheriff's words.

"Miriam Hunter, you have the right to remain silent...."

NINE

"What do you mean the package was gone?" Owen asked the back of Wes's head from the top step of Miriam's basement stairs.

"Like I said, we looked on every rock out there. Nada. No package and no sign of a flying bicycle."

"So there you go. From the time I brought Miriam back to when you got out there, the pickup of the package was completed by the real perp. That proves her innocence."

Wes led Owen to a wooden door that matched the surface of the walls. He wouldn't have known the door was there if Wes hadn't pulled it open. "It proves nothing. Besides, this is all the proof I need."

He pulled a string dangling in front of them. Light revealed an eight-by-eight room filled with tan stacks of plastic-wrapped rectangular blocks from floor to ceiling.

Marijuana.

"I knew she was involved all along," Wes exclaimed as Owen walked the perimeter of the room, forced to accept the sight before him—and what it would mean for Miriam. "She and her interpreter friend thought they were so hilarious, making fun of me right in front of my face. Well, now who's laughing?"

Owen's brain went into overdrive. "Nick said he had an appointment he couldn't miss. Maybe he went to retrieve the package. Maybe he snuck these in here when Miriam wasn't home. I'm sure she doesn't even know this room exists."

"Why are you defending her?" Wes demanded. "She's guilty, Owen. Look around you. Just because she's disabled doesn't mean the laws are different for her."

Disabled. It was the same word Owen had used with Miriam less than hour ago, but hearing it from Wes's mouth sounded a bit harsh. It made him wonder how she felt when she heard people say it. How it made her feel when he'd said it to her. A stir of his scruples told him he might have hurt her.

"Oh, man, I think I messed up," Owen mumbled aloud. He spoke to himself but also to Wes. "I think we might be wrong about that. I've watched her thrive in her surroundings with no assistance from anyone. Yes, she needs an interpreter, but anyone who speaks a different language would. That doesn't make her disabled, right?"

Wes folded his arms, his head bouncing. "Oh, I see how it is. Never would I have believed it, but it seems I've uncovered two secrets today. It's too bad you've fallen for a drug smuggler," he huffed. "This would kill Rebecca all over again. Unless you're glad she's gone so you and the fiery redhead can get together."

Wes's remark drove the air from Owen's lungs. He could do nothing but stand among the stacks of the destructive, toxic drug and hear the echo of his friend's words, just as potent.

"I asked you to come here to help me crack this case," Wes continued. "I did not expect you to interfere with it by getting cozy with the number-one suspect. You may not think too much of this island, but I do. It's been my home all my life, and I will protect it from outsiders who only want to abuse it for their own gain."

"And that's what you think Miriam is about? Harming your precious island?" Owen pushed his fists into his waist to keep them from slamming into Wes's face. "All Miriam wanted was to be a part of this community. To belong here. Did you even try to talk to her? Maybe learn a little bit of her language so you could say hi, how are you? Or did you avoid her instead?"

"Don't you try to turn this on me. Look around you, Owen. The evidence is in *her* house."

"Yes, but did you look for leads anywhere else? Or were you so focused on getting rid of her that perhaps you overlooked some other people? People who might have planted this stuff here for the same reason you're going after her. I told you Nick has been misinterpreting her words. Miriam's a funny lady, but I'm sure a lot of the jokes you think she said were Nick doing his best to ruin her."

"Nick? I doubt that. They're friends."

"Some friend. I'm actually not surprised the whole town has turned against her. Because of him, they think she's evil and rude."

Wes rubbed along his jaw in indecision, staring at the rows of drugs. "I don't have any other leads, but maybe I didn't look deep enough into Nick Danforth." He faced Owen. "All right, listen. I'm not willing to let her go just yet. But I won't put her on the ferry tomorrow to be arraigned in Bangor, either. She can stay at the clinic this week while I do a little more snooping into Nick's past."

"Can you get rid of the handcuffs?"

"It's either handcuffs or the holding cell."

"You might as well gag her mouth. Her hands are the way she communicates."

Wes shook his head. "I don't have a spare man to guard her."

"I'll guard her. It'll be my badge and gun if I don't."

Wes's cheek twitched, but he reached into his pocket and withdrew a key ring. His thick fingers worked at removing a key, and he placed it in

Owen's waiting hand. "You must really like her if you're willing to give everything up if she runs."

"It's not like you think." He pocketed it. "We're friends. That's it. But I trust her, and I know she didn't do this." He gestured to the stacks of marijuana. "I can see now why someone wanted her out of here. By moving in, she disrupted their operation."

"You're jumping to a lot of conclusions, Owen."

"You're not jumping to enough."

"All I know is we've never had illegal drugs on this island until Ms. Hunter and Mr. Danforth showed up."

"Perhaps they were released as a way to get rid of her. Without her here to live in this house, it would stay vacant for a long time. Makes a great holding place before distribution to the pushers, I'd say."

"Perhaps, but someone would buy the house eventually."

"Has anyone made an offer or said they would like first dibs?"

Wes grew quiet, not recalling any names. It felt as though he didn't want to answer.

"Well?" Owen asked again. "Has there been an offer?"

Wes cleared his throat. "Frank Thibodaux said he wanted it for his family. So what? He was Hans's best friend. No one around here is going to deny an old man and fellow islander a final wish. We take care of our own."

"It seems to me all roads lead to Frank Thibodaux around here."

"Owen, you'd better watch your step." A dangerous edge to Wes's voice caused Owen to eye his friend dead-on.

"Is that some kind of warning?"

"Like I said. My job is to protect the people of this island from outsiders."

Owen nodded, reading the message loud and clear. At the end of the day, he was one of those outsiders.

Owen didn't want to think the worst of his friend, but he needed to know to what extremes Wes would take his job. To the point of scaring an unwanted outsider away? Would he even plant evidence to bring the law down on her so she was sent to be imprisoned on the mainland and off his precious island? And if that failed, would he attempt to kill her?

"Let me out, Mother! I won't sign anymore." Miriam hoped she said the words correctly. Speaking was so hard for her. Making her lips move the right way, then dragging air up from her tummy to blow out felt funny. But not as funny as the way people looked at her when she tried. She had no idea how she sounded, but when she got a scrunched-up face

like the person ate a lemon, Miriam knew she'd got it wrong.

She hated that look. It made her feel dumb.

I'm not dumb. *Coach Erin told her those were Helen Keller's first spoken words to the hearing world. And she'd also told her that Miriam wasn't dumb, either. Coach said that she was just speaking the wrong language. And then Coach showed her the right one.*

But now, with her hands tied in front of her, Miriam could speak no more. She tried her hardest to sit still on the cold hard floor in Grandma Trudy's dark basement.

I hate the dark. I can't see anything. It makes me feel so small. Even though I'm a little girl, it makes me feel like I'm even smaller, like I'm not here anymore.

Miriam wondered how long her punishment would last this time.

She struggled up from the ground, using her bound hands as leverage. Breath lodged in Miriam's chest, squeezing it to the point that only a streamline of air passed through. With her chin up, Miriam faced the door she knew was above her. Even if she couldn't see it, she knew it was there at the top of the stairs. She couldn't say the same for the areas around her, and she had to force her head to face the unknown darkness.

Her chin trembled as she peered over her right

shoulder. Slowly she twisted her rigid body around, but she dared not move in any direction.

Her body shook and she wished she could wrap her arms around her shoulders to get warm. The straps of her sundress did nothing to block the cold breeze blowing over her from her right.

Miriam wondered where the cold air came from, but she also wanted to get away from it. The darkness on her left seemed different, not as dark as her right. And not as cold. Like to a bug at night, life-giving light, warmth and safety beckoned her forward.

She put one foot in front of the other and bumped along cool rock walls. She was in some kind of passageway like the ones in the castles of her fairy tales. Miriam stubbed her big toe on something sharp, leaving her sandal sticky. She ignored it, for the pathway grew brighter ahead.

Light burned around the next bend. Miriam's steps picked up speed. The light was a magnet, and she was powerless to its attraction. Her feet carried her at full speed into a small room, and instantly she could breathe better. She didn't feel so small anymore.

Shadows danced merrily on rock walls. A candle flickered on a wooden table in the middle of the room. Miriam stepped in farther, scanning the dancing shadows around her.

Except they weren't all shadows. A real person

sat in a chair against the far wall. It was a lady, and her eyes bulged as they looked at Miriam.

Miriam's legs locked, suddenly not liking this place at all. The woman's eyes were so big. So scary.

Miriam backed away, but something yanked her wrist. She noticed a big hand in front of her eyes, pulling up her tied arms. Up and up the big, white knuckles pulled. Pain cut into her as the scene flashed gold and black.

And then out.

A sharp tug on her right hand jolted Miriam from her sleep. Her eyes opened wide to fluorescent lamp–lit clinical surroundings and settled on the hand holding her cuffed wrist. Fingers curled around her skin like the ones from her dream. The same dream she'd had since she was ten years old. And every time she had it, she'd swear it was real.

Especially with the hand still holding her.

Her gaze rose from the grip to meet the face it belonged to.

Owen.

Her brain tripped over this information. Was he the man from her dreams? She looked at his hand again to compare it.

Owen's fingers were longer, thinner. His knuckles weren't big and white and didn't protrude in their grasp like the hand that had grabbed her with a vengeance. Miriam could rest assured; Owen Matthews was not the man from her dreams.

Something silver flashed between the fingers of his other hand. He brought it over the handcuffs that chained her to the bed. With a twist of his hand, the cuffs opened and slid from her wrist.

Air rushed into her lungs as she realized she was free again. Free because of Owen. He might not be the man from her dreams, but at the moment, he sure was the man *of* her dreams.

She took in his dark brooding eyes as she rubbed away the residual discomfort left by the cuffs. He swallowed hard, making his neck contract, and tossed the cuffs on the bedside table without removing his eyes from her. *So serious,* she thought. Not the look of a man here to set her free, after all.

But maybe a reprieve? "Thank you," she signed, able to speak once again.

"I hated seeing Wes slap these on you." Owen sighed deeply. "He's letting me guard you here instead of inside a jail cell, but you're still in a lot of trouble, Miriam. I saw the drugs in your basement myself. But even so, I told him he's wrong about you."

She tilted her head, comparing Owen's words with his opinion of her from earlier. "Because a disabled person couldn't be capable of such things?"

Dark eyes drooped with remorse. "I'm so sorry I said that. I have no excuse but ignorance. These last few days with you have shown me I have a lot to learn." He flashed his dimple in a sheepish grin. "But I couldn't think of a better teacher—or principal—to do the teaching."

Miriam's lips twitched. With Owen's heart-melting charms turned on her, she found it increasingly difficult to stay mad at him. Besides, he was willing to learn, and what principal would ever turn away a willing student?

"I brought my video TTY phone for you to use." Owen signaled to the chair behind him, where the machine rested. "You get one phone call like everyone else, and it should be on a phone useful to you." He could kick Wes for not supplying one for her. The fact that the sheriff didn't have one on hand in case the island's deaf resident needed to contact the police really upset him, but Owen would curtail his disappointment at his friend for now. Clearing an innocent woman's name took precedence.

Owen placed the screen on the bedside table while observing Miriam's mood change. He was glad to see the petrified expression on her face had been replaced with her infectiously sweet smile again. When he'd first awakened her, her dull hue and deep-set eyes had made him feel as if he were the enemy. As if she expected him to harm her.

Then he thought maybe he was the enemy. His guilt at his earlier ignorance told him his words had been just as harmful as any weapon. And yet Miriam forgave him without question. And rewarded him with her clean-slate eyes and beaming smile.

Even though she was the one under arrest.

Now her hands were the focus of her attention. While Owen plugged in the phone cord, she wrung them the way a hearing person might worry on their lower lip when they were at a loss for words.

Something had made Miriam Hunter speechless.

Was her arrest finally sinking in? Owen assured her he would get to the bottom of it. What if he couldn't, though? How could he promise her anything at this point? The drugs were in her house. The fact is he should be telling her to use her one phone call for an attorney.

"So who do you want to call?" he asked instead.

She shook her head and waved the phone away from her.

"No one?" he signed. "Not a family member or friend?"

"I don't have any family, and my closest friend is somewhere on the island."

Owen contemplated his next words. "How about your mother?"

Miriam's gray eyes flashed dark before resettling with her nonchalant shrug. "Not necessary. We don't...talk anymore." Owen didn't miss the fact that Miriam used the sign for *talk* instead of *sign*.

He curbed his tongue from asking why and reached to turn off the machine.

Miriam touched his forearm. Her fingers seared him instantly. The feeling must be growing on him, though, because when she withdrew it, he covered the place to hold in her warmth.

"I changed my mind. I know who I want to call." Her hands moved in a blurry haze.

"Great." He forced his hand to engage. "Who?"

"Your son."

"What?" Owen cut her a quick glance, speaking out loud and forgetting to sign.

"I want to call Cole."

Both his hands and lips refused to move now.

"Please." The color of clean slate beckoned from her eyes. It reminded him of the chalkboard he'd scrawled Shakespeare's sonnet on. A surface that could be easily cleaned.

It would take more than an eraser—and a pretty girl—to wipe his sins away.

Miriam scooted up in the bed, smoothing down the lapel of her white robe. She directed that look of acceptance at him again that made him think he just might give her the world.

Owen's fingers automatically punched out the number to Rebecca's parents.

Rebecca's father answered, but within seconds Cole appeared and filled the screen with his pale blond looks. A curious expression widened his blue eyes as he waited for his dad to speak.

"Hi, Cole," Owen signed stiffly, spelling out his name, but by the time he reached the letter *E,* Owen's fingers trailed off. More than anything, he wanted to give his son one of those special name signs that Miriam had mentioned. Something that would suit his character. But then he figured it should come from someone who knew Cole better, so, instead, Owen turned the screen to include Miriam.

"Who are you?" Cole signed and brought his face up close and personal to the camera's lens.

"I'm Miriam." She spelled out her own name, but also gave him her name sign. "Your dad is helping me at my school."

"You sign? Are you deaf?"

"I am deaf just like you. Your dad has told me so much about you."

Owen stepped back out of the picture and wondered why she'd said that. It wasn't true. He could barely talk to Cole, never mind about him.

From his point behind the screen he couldn't see Cole's answer, only Miriam's replies. It seemed to him everything she said was about him, as though she deliberately painted him in a good light. An undeserving light.

"I understand," she signed. "I sometimes feel lonely, too. But your grandparents sound really nice. Plus, if I had a phone like this, I don't think I would be lonely anymore. You're very lucky to have a dad who gave you a videophone. This is so cool. I am going to buy one tomorrow."

Her smile was infectious. "You can have this one," Owen signed on impulse.

Her face lit up like a Fourth of July sky, which made his spontaneous gift worth it. "Your dad just said I could have this one. Can you believe it? He's so nice."

Owen thought she was trying too hard, but he let her continue with her attempt at bonding father and son. He didn't have the heart to tell her it was pointless.

"Of course I'll call you again. I'm going to love using my new phone. I wish I'd had one of these before. It's so much easier and nicer to sign directly to a person, rather than typing in a message."

Owen wondered if she would use the phone as she said. If she didn't have anyone to call to tell them about the trouble she was in now, then why would she have someone to call later?

"Really? Getting this phone was your idea because you like cameras? I bet you talk to your dad all the time on it."

Her smile drooped at the edges. Her facial muscles strained to keep it there for Cole's sake. "I'm sorry, Cole. Parents don't always get it right." She peered over the screen. "I think your dad loves you very much but doesn't know how to say it."

Owen escaped farther back until the chair bumped him from behind. An obstacle that blocked his path to the door? Or forced him to face the firing squad?

"I think that's a great idea!" Miriam clapped her hands in enthusiasm, then threw her strong, swimmer's legs over the edge of the bed. She patted the place beside her to invite him to sit.

She wanted him be a part of this conversation?

He could barely breathe.

"Come. Your son wants to teach you something. And you did say you were willing to learn. So park it. School's in session."

Owen shook his head, but when her hand reached for him, he latched on like a drowning victim. She had to peel his fingers from her hand so she could continue to speak.

"Go ahead, Cole."

Cole took a deep breath, his tiny shoulders lifted in preparation. He pushed his blond hair out of his sky-blue eyes and leaned in toward the camera again. "Are you ready, Dad?"

Owen hesitated, not sure what he needed to be ready for and thought facing criminals with guns was easier than facing his child.

Miriam elbowed him in the rib cage; her eyes flashed a warning that made him think he would take those criminals over her any day, too. "I'm ready."

"I." Cole pointed his pinky up and stopped.

Miriam nudged Owen again, prompting him to repeat after his son.

"I," he mimicked.

"Love." Cole crossed his fisted arms at his chest, but it felt more like a fist to Owen's gut.

"Love." Owen's arms shook as he did the same.

"You." Cole pointed straight at the camera, his little finger taking up half the screen.

Owen raised his trembling hand, reaching for his son.

"No," Cole signed. "You're doing it wrong. It's just one finger. You were right, Miriam. He doesn't know how to say it."

Owen's laugh hitched with an emotion other than humor, and he had to choke down tears lodged at the back of his throat. "I think she's right about a lot of things." Owen angled a look in her direction.

Owen may have been holding back the tears, but Miriam wasn't. Her eyes brimmed with glistening moisture until one tear made its escape.

Owen caught it with his thumb as he cupped the side of her smooth freckled face.

She encircled her fingers around his and with a squeeze pushed it to his lap. "Before we hang up, we have one more thing to talk about, and it's really important."

Owen tensed. What could she be planning to tell Cole? Was she going to bring up his mother?

Owen shook his head to stop her from saying anything else.

She ignored him. "Cole, we need to give you a name sign."

Trapped breath squeezed out of Owen's lungs as Miriam asked Cole questions about things he liked to do, toys he liked to play with and his favorite foods.

Owen touched her hand to interrupt. "I have a sign that might work," he signed tentatively.

"Really?" both Cole and Miriam replied, their expressions expectant and excited.

"Yes." Doubt grew in Owen. "If you don't want to keep it, we can give you another one."

"Of course he'll want it. It's more special when it comes from someone who loves you."

His hands shook. "I was thinking since Cole likes cameras, especially video cameras, I thought the letter *C* cranking the side of a video camera would fit him." Owen curled his hand into a *C* and demonstrated the sign, then shifted uneasily.

Cole jumped up and down, his face one big smile, looking so much like any other young boy his age. Owen felt relief that his sign had been accepted. But shame quickly followed. For so long, Owen had refused to see the boy before the deafness.

Another thing he needed to repent for. Another thing his son would have to forgive him for…or not.

"I love it, and I love you, Dad!" Cole's exuberant

expression filled the screen again. Owen searched for the judgment that stared at him from the mirror every morning. He knew it had to be there behind the words that tugged on his heart and tricked him into believing he was forgiven.

Instead, an innocent face stared back. Hope showed from the screen. All Owen could see was a boy who needed his father. Not one looking for restitution.

How could he withhold anything from Cole anymore? How could he make Cole pay for the sins of the father any longer? "I love you, Cole." Owen used the newly appointed name sign that felt so right.

"Your signing is getting better," Cole signed with excitement. "Keep practicing, Dad. And then I can come live with you."

Owen's throat tightened. "No, Cole. You need to stay with Grandma and Grandpa. They can take care of you better."

"Why?"

"I just told you. You need to listen."

"I was right. You don't love me. You lied." Cole's signing hands punctuated his growing anger. He reached at the screen with scrunched lips, then the screen went blank. He'd clicked off.

Miriam had never seen guilty students retreat faster from her office than Owen's retreat from her. He put away the phone in heavy silence. Taking extra care and time in winding the cord up, he focused on that instead of on her. She wondered if he was angry at her for forcing him into the conversation with Cole, or if he was angry at his son.

She hoped it was her. She could handle that. Miriam wasn't so sure about the alternative. She prayed Owen's situation with his son wasn't a repeat of her own relationship with her mother.

Miriam had thought in the beginning of the phone call that Owen didn't feel worthy to be part of the conversation. That for some reason he lacked confidence in relating to his child, not that there was animosity between them.

The ending of the call told her otherwise.

The principal in her stepped up to the plate. Parents played a critical role in their child's education. A parent is a child's first and most important teacher. If a gap existed between the child and parent, learning would be extremely difficult for the child throughout their life. And Cole, especially because of his deafness, needed the support and encouragement that could only come from his father.

But before Miriam could intercede between father and son, she would need to know the truth of how Owen felt about his son's deafness. She prayed she would be able to handle the answer.

She would also need to get his attention.

Miriam snapped her fingers, a gesture she found kind of rude but sometimes necessary if someone purposely tuned her out. Besides, it usually did the trick, and seeing Owen's dark eyes target her, this time was no different.

She lifted her hands to sign, "Your son needs you."

"He needs someone safe." Owen's hands flew angrily as he answered her. "Someone who will be there for him. I have a job that puts me in danger daily. I sent Cole to his grandparents' for a reason. If something happens to me out on the field, he won't be hurt too much."

"He's hurting now." Her hands stilled for a moment while she studied Owen's taut face. "And so are you."

"I should be hurting more."

"Why? I don't understand."

Owen turned his back on her, a simple movement that effectively tuned her out again. His navy blue T-shirt stretched across his back. She could see his shoulder muscles tense beneath the fabric, working through a problem he wished the strength of his body could take care of.

But certain problems needed something other than body strength. They needed the use of a different part of the body that tended to be overlooked more times than not.

The heart.

Miriam put her feet down onto the cold tile and padded up to his side, brushing his arm.

She came around and placed her left hand on his chest. Beneath her fingers, his heart beat a rapid cadence. It spoke volumes to her. It spoke of a fight within in him that he battled daily—and was losing.

Please, Father, don't let Cole's deafness be the cause of Owen's fight.

"Why are you hurting?" She lifted her hands from his chest to sign.

Owen's lips twisted in defiance. His hands remained still.

"Please. Talk to me." Miriam couldn't wait any longer. She needed an answer to the question that had plagued her her whole life. "Is having a deaf child really so bad?"

"Yes." Owen's answer came quick and swift.

Miriam flinched, but the normal anger that rolled so close to the surface when she denied this to be true didn't spring up. Instead a dull pain resonated through her, from her heart to her head, and straight down her arms to her fingertips.

Miriam dropped her shoulders and her gaze to her open hands. To the things that made her look like a freak. *I guess Mother was right after all.*

Miriam didn't want to believe it was true, but maybe it was time to accept it. To stop fighting the hearing world's view that she was flawed. That there was something wrong with her.

Miriam filled her stomach with air and pushed words from her mouth. "I…see." She spoke through her mouth. At Owen's surprise, Miriam figured she sounded just as freaky, but she opened her mouth and pushed out, "I did not realize…deaf children… caused so much pain…to their parents. I thought it was…just my mother."

"Why are you talking?" Owen signed, his face swamped with confusion.

"Isn't that…what you want?"

"No!" Owen's hands flashed quickly in her face.

"Your son's deafness…hurts you. That must be the same for…me."

"My son's deafness hurts me because I caused it!" Owen's face was mottled in red.

Miriam's lips sealed shut. *Owen caused his son's deafness?* Her mind tried to process that. "How?" she signed her natural language automatically.

Owen dragged a hand down his face. Would he decide not to answer her? Miriam stepped closer and gently took his hand away from his face. She implored him in silence, patting his hand to urge him to speak to her.

Owen squeezed her hand, then withdrew to sign. "I caused Cole's deafness, and I caused my wife's death. Six years ago I took her and Cole out on a boat that I knew hadn't passed safety inspections. It needed new bulbs, among other things, but I took it out anyway. I thought it was no big deal. I knew what I was doing and where I was going, so who cared? Except I wasn't counting on a storm coming down on us. It blew us way off course, and it took hours to get back. By then it was dark." Owen's hands began to shake. He squeezed his fists tightly, halting him from going further.

Miriam covered his quaking fists, praying for God to help Owen in his darkness. She closed her eyes and silently called on her Father to lend His righteous right hand to Owen's life.

After a few minutes, Owen's hands calmed and Miriam opened her eyes. She let go of his hands so he could continue.

"I saw a boat coming at us. It had its lights on. I flashed mine, but they didn't work. I could see the other boat, but they couldn't see me. I tried to steer out of the way, but they were too close and…we collided." Owen dropped down on the chair's edge, cradling the sides of his head with his hands for a few moments. "Rebecca paid for my arrogance and stupidity with her life. Cole paid with his hearing after nearly drowning. And I walked away." His stiff face rose defiantly to her. "That's why Cole's deafness pains me. It's my fault. All my fault."

Miriam shook her head and dropped to her knees in front of him. Their foreheads touched, and Miriam searched the dark eyes that had hidden his secret for six years. A secret that ate at him and kept him from a relationship with his son—and most likely from God, too.

Miriam breathed deeply, knowing Owen didn't

reject his son because he was deaf after all. He just didn't believe he was worthy of a relationship with Cole because of his actions.

Miriam pulled back a few inches. Just enough to tell him the truth. "I'm so sorry you've gone through this, but Cole doesn't blame you."

"He should hate me," Owen signed viciously.

"He will if you keep rejecting him. Trust me." Miriam placed her hand over her heart for a few beats. "He will go through his life believing you are rejecting him because he is deaf."

Owen's expression became quizzical. He searched her face before settling on her eyes. His hand rose to her cheek and he rubbed a thumb gently down the side of her face. "I don't deserve this," he said. She read his lips clearly. He lifted his hands and signed, "It should have been me. I deserve to die. A life for a life."

Miriam shook her head adamantly and signed, "No! Christ gave His life so all our debts are paid. He bled so you don't have to. It's done. Ask for forgiveness, and you will be forgiven. Accept this gift from God. Accept God."

Owen moved away from her. A mixture of emotions played across his face—desire to believe her, old guilt to stop him. Owen retreated to the darkness of his soul. It appeared he didn't believe in God's forgiving love.

But Miriam could always count on God to find

her, even in the darkest of places. No place was too dark for Him. He saw her clearly as though it was the brightest of days. He'd found her in the dark before, and He would find Owen in his dark place, too.

"God's waiting for you to hear Him. He wants to help you understand, but you've tuned His voice out."

"What do you know about His voice?"

"He speaks my language. Listen to Him, Owen. He will speak yours, too. And He will help you escape the darkness you are in. He's done it for me."

"Really? And when you get sent to jail, is He going to help you escape then, too? Because you're in a heap of trouble right now, and I don't see Him showing up to clear your name or to save you from someone who wants you dead."

She expelled a breath and scooted back. "Whatever happens, I will trust God to strengthen me and guide me through it. He's made that promise—to both of us. Try to listen to the message He has for you. That's all I'm asking." She rested her hand on her chest.

"The only thing I want to hear right now is Frank Thibodaux's take on the current circumstances." He stood and grabbed the handcuffs.

"You have to handcuff me again?" she signed her question with slumped shoulders.

He nodded his answer. "I have to call in to a judge I know on the mainland for an ROR. A release on your own recognizance. But until then, I have to handcuff you if I leave. I'm sorry."

"Don't be. I know it's not your doing," she signed, then went back to her bed and gave him her right hand willingly. But instead of taking it, Owen pointed to her left.

At her confusion, he signed, "It's bad enough Wes has taken away your freedom. I won't let him take away your voice, too."

Heat flushed Miriam's skin to the point she barely felt the cold metal cinch her wrist. Her mind exploded in an uproar even she could hear. A flux of sensation at this man's understanding coursed through her veins, heading straight to her heart.

Miriam absorbed the presence of the cuff weighing down her left hand, locking her to her bed again. But that wasn't the weight that quieted her hands.

She thought it might be an overwhelming feeling of love, but she had to be mistaken. She had to be confusing love with gratitude. Owen's thoughtful gesture to leave her right hand free so she could speak endeared him to her, but that didn't mean she wanted to jump off the cliff of love.

It couldn't be love. That was one ledge she had to talk herself off. And yet, somewhere deep inside, she could already feel herself beginning to fall.

TEN

The classy, subdued environment of the Blue Lobster caught Owen by surprise. After his robust experience at the Underground Küchen, he expected the dinner hour on the opposite end of the boardwalk to be a similar experience.

"Table for one?" A dark-haired woman approached him with a menu. Her white blouse and black pants were creased with precision to all their refined points and lines. She floated by tables with fine linens and crystal flutes.

No flouncy aprons would be found in this high-end establishment. An establishment that most likely cost a pretty penny to run and might need to be subsidized with something on the side.

Like illegal drug trafficking.

"Yes, it's only me," Owen answered the waitress. "I'm new to the island and haven't made many friends yet."

"Oh, you must be the new teacher." She led him

to a table by the bay window. The setting sun's rays sparkled on the overturned glasses.

In his jeans and T-shirt, he felt a little under-dressed to be on display. So much for blending in. "Actually, do you have something in the back? A little more private?" he asked.

"Um…" The young woman peered over her shoulder. "There's a meeting going on in the back room, but I suppose I could seat you at the back wall. Would that be better?"

"That would be perfect." Especially if it put him within hearing distance of that meeting.

She led the way and stopped right outside a room where a group of men sat around a table. "I should tell you that you'll be alone back here. If you're looking to make friends that might be hard to do in this spot." She bit her lower lip, looking as though she had more to say.

"And?" Owen coaxed her.

She flashed a tentative smile. "Well, I have a break coming. I could sit and keep you company."

Owen hesitated in giving his normal outright refusal he used when a woman clued him in on her interest. Typically, he hated leading someone on, but in this instance, he weighed the costs versus the benefits. This woman might have some pertinent information on the owner that he could draw out of her with little to no effort.

"I'm Rachelle, by the way. Rachelle Thibodaux.

My grandfather owns the place," she willingly offered, proving his point already. "So I won't get fired, if that's what you're worried about."

"Well, I really would hate to get you into any trouble. Jobs are hard to come by." He took his seat and pushed the glass away.

"Is that why you came to the island?" She placed an opened menu down in front of him. "The job market tough in... I'm sorry—where did you say you were from?"

Owen held her coy gaze. The polished young woman had just turned the tables on him. It seemed Frank Thibodaux had himself a real family-oriented enterprise.

Owen thought back to Ben Thibodaux's statement. *"I need to graduate and get off this island. Otherwise, I won't have anything to look forward to but a life of doing someone else's bidding."* Judging by the stark fear Owen had seen in Ben's eyes that day when asked, "Whose bidding?"...the boy feared someone. Was it his grandfather?

"I came in from the border," Owen vaguely answered Rachelle's question about where he was from. "And as much as I would like the pleasure of your company tonight, it's kind of a working dinner for me."

"Oh, of course." She shrugged nonchalantly. "I'm actually not surprised. I've heard the new principal's a slave driver."

An image of Miriam's elegantly expressive face materialized. She sure was getting under his skin, and not because she was a slave driver. "Ms. Hunter's actually very nice." If only these people would give Miriam a few moments. They would see the kindness in her. They would see a heart filled with love and compassion, especially for their children. "Stepping Stones should get to know her better before making a judgment."

"I suppose you're right. It's... I don't know, it's hard to communicate with her, I guess. I feel like she won't understand, so why bother?"

"You bother because she's a person. She wants to belong like everyone else. She has feelings that get hurt like everyone else, too. If you traveled to another country and didn't speak the language, would that mean you were less of a person than the natives?"

"No, but I would try to learn the language."

"Well, that's great if you can hear it."

Rachelle dropped her gaze to her hands. "I guess that's something to think about."

"And while you're thinking, learning a few signs won't hurt. Might even help break the ice with Ms. Hunter."

Rachelle shot a quick look into the room before whispering, "Do you know any?"

Owen came to an impasse. If he admitted to knowing sign language, he would blow his cover.

The buzz would go out as fast as a flock of seagulls and could alert the wrong people, sending them packing. If that happened, there would be no way to clear Miriam's name.

He couldn't let her take the fall for these crimes, but he also couldn't miss this opportunity to help her find her place among the islanders.

Miriam hadn't told him the particulars of her childhood, but Owen got the gist that she still had a lot of pain deep inside her. And not belonging on this island cut her even deeper.

Owen made his decision. Her pain won out. If he chose his words carefully, he could continue to clear her name while building a few bridges for her. "I know a bit of sign language that could help you at least say 'hi' and 'I want to be friends.' Do you want to try? You might find it fun."

Rachelle stepped closer, blocking Owen's view of the inhabitants in the room. Blocking Owen's view or blocking the inhabitants' view? He wasn't so sure if Rachelle was a complete devotee to the Thibodaux family's cause, but he was grateful for her covering.

Owen slowly signed, "Hi, I'm Rachelle. I want to be friends."

She smiled as she tried the signs and laughed at her confusion and mess-ups, but she didn't give up and tried again. She laughed some more. "I sure hope Ms. Hunter's forgiving."

Rachelle's words struck him. Miriam's gray eyes

came to mind. "Amazingly so," Owen confirmed with a tightening throat.

"What are you laughing about, Rachelle?" a deep baritone called from the doorway to the room.

"Oh, Uncle Jerome, I'm sorry. I didn't mean to disturb you. I was chatting with the new teacher." She shifted to reveal Owen's presence.

"Owen! Buddy! How you doing?" Jerome stepped to the table and turned a chair to straddle it.

The image felt abrasive in such a refined atmosphere. It must irk Frank to have a son so crude. No wonder he was at the Underground Küchen the other day. He probably wasn't allowed to eat here.

"Fine. I thought I'd check out the competition for dinner tonight." Owen said. "I hope Rachelle and I didn't interrupt anything too important."

"Nah." Jerome waved the hand with the fat black-and-gold ring at Owen. "My dad got wind of some problems with the new principal and he called a family meeting." He thumbed at Rachelle to move along, which she did.

"There's a problem with my boss?" Owen acted surprised as he watched Rachelle go behind the bar. He could see her practicing her letters for her name and he smiled within.

"Yeah, it seems she's involved with the growing drug problem."

"You're kidding. I don't believe it. Ms. Hunter? Are you sure?" Owen stretched back on his chair's hind legs. The quality of the furniture told him it would hold him as he played the part of Jerome's equal.

"Mightily." Jerome leaned in and whispered behind the back of his hand. "Caught red-handed with half a mil."

Owen bulged out his eyes for effect, while he wondered how Jerome would have come by such information—unless he was the owner of the product. Owen brought his legs down slowly and whispered, "Is that a lot of money?"

"Is that a lot?" Jerome threw his head back and chuckled. "Boy, you gotta get your head out of those fancy books. Yeah, it's a lot."

"Will someone come looking for their money soon?"

A pasty hue broke out on Jerome's neck and cheeks. Perhaps Jerome experienced a little anxiety over the idea of collection day encroaching.

Jerome bolted out of his chair before Owen could determine. "Come on. I'll introduce you to the family."

The table in the back room held five men and a teenager. Owen zeroed in on the one familiar face: Ben Thibodaux. He sat next to the patriarch, whose eyes were cast down to avoid Owen's as though he was a cruise liner and Owen was one of the stepping stones.

"Hey," Jerome said. "This is Owen Matthews, the new teacher at the school."

A man stood, leaner but older than Jerome. Gray hairs speckled his short black cut. His hand reached for Owen. "Hello, Mr. Matthews. Len speaks highly of you. I'm Alec, head of custodial engineering at the school."

Right, the janitor that doesn't like to be called a janitor, Owen thought as he accepted Alec's handshake. "Nice to meet you, and I'll bc sure to thank Len later, too. I was actually intrigued to learn about his not-so-secret passageway. Any of you ever been inside?"

He focused on the very old man sitting with his back to the wall, surrounded by his sons and grandsons. Owen felt guilty speculating if the man was packing a gun in his double-breasted suit. He did not look long for this world, with his yellowed, sunken face. He was obviously deathly ill. This very well could be his last meal.

But if Frank wasn't packing, was Jerome or Alec? Or the other two men at the table?

Or worse, Ben?

Owen's stomach rolled at the thought of this seventeen-year-old boy wielding a gun, but in his line of work, Owen had come up against kids who'd cut their teeth on guns. They were something to fear because to them, killing for the family was accepted as a part of everyday life.

"Yes, Mr. Matthews, I have been in Len's passageway," Frank spoke with a rattle, and Alec retook his seat. "They were supposedly carved out by pirates that inhabited the island long ago. A place to hide their plunder, as the stories go. I also have a passageway of my own, but it was boarded up years ago after a little problem occurred." The old man's jowls swayed as he glanced at Jerome. "I received word the tunnel was being used inappropriately. So, I'm sorry if you were looking for a tour of mine, because that's not going to be possible at this time."

Owen wasn't looking for a tour, but the fact that Frank also had a passageway made him question if the Hunter home had one, too. He couldn't see how Hans would have been the odd man out of the three without one.

And if there was one, then Owen would have his alternative route for getting the drugs in and the start of a case of defense for Miriam. The fact that his job wasn't about searching for defensive strategies for people but rather for cases of guilt didn't go unnoticed. He chalked it up to not wanting to put an innocent person behind bars, but the truth nipping at his heels said it was for an entirely different reason—that Miriam Hunter was coming to mean more to him than a case to solve.

"Can I be excused?" Ben asked his grandfather under his breath but loud enough to be heard by all.

"Is there a problem? Do you not get along with

your new teacher?" Frank asked and lifted a gnarled hand in Owen's direction. Owen thought if the man was carrying a gun, it would be because of a death wish. Owen would be able to get ten shots off before the old man even lifted his gun.

"No," Ben mumbled. "I have homework to do."

Frank nodded once, and the boy pushed away from the table for a clean retreat.

"Hey, Ben." Owen stopped him at the back exit. "Can I speak with you for second? I actually wanted to ask you about the lesson we were discussing this week. Do you mind?"

"Does he mind?" Jerome's voice broke the silence. "Owen, I would be much obliged if you could set my son on the right track. Any little bit you can offer to get him to graduation day would put me forever in your debt."

Ben jammed his hands deep into his black jeans pockets. "Sure, whatever." He exited through the back door.

Owen addressed the group as he followed Ben out. "Sorry I have to cut out so quickly, but I don't want to miss this opportunity to help Ben. I don't get to talk with him at school much."

"Not a prob, Owen," Jerome assured him. "He's a tough one to crack. I appreciate you wanting to help. I wish other teachers had cared as much as you. Maybe then he wouldn't be such a troublemaker."

The door slammed on Jerome's words.

Owen searched through the dark night for the man's son. Lamps lit the boardwalk, casting dark shadows of hiding spaces every ten feet. Ben could be standing in any one of them or none at all. He could have snuck into an alley and disappeared.

After witnessing the Thibodaux family gathering, Owen felt Ben was the leak he needed to crack this case.

Except now he was gone.

"What do you want?" Ben's voice spoke from behind him. Owen whipped around to find the boy hidden on the side of the building.

Owen stepped closer. "I want to help you."

"Help me? You're no teacher. You can't help me."

"Why do you think I'm not a teacher?"

"I saw you signing. You're a cop, aren't you? Sent here to work with the principal to investigate who's pushing the drugs, right?"

Owen judged how much truth to share. He needed to build trust with Ben, and lying would push him further away. "Regardless of what I am, I do want to help you, whether it is in the classroom or out. I mean that."

"You want to help me? Make her leave. If she just went away, then none of this would have to happen." Ben slipped into the darkness.

"Wait! Ben! What has to happen?" Owen rushed forward.

Ben emerged under the lamplight. "Tell me one thing, *Teacher*. How do I sign, 'I'm sorry'?"

Stumped, Owen demonstrated the simple sign of a circling fist at chest level. He wondered when Ben planned to use the sign—and why. Was something coming that he would need Miriam's forgiveness for?

"That's it?" Ben scoffed. "It seems like asking for forgiveness should be harder than a circling fist. You should have to bleed." With that he stepped back and fused with the darkness again. This time, he didn't reappear.

Owen looked at his still-curled fist hanging in front of him. Miriam's words flashed back at him. *"Christ gave His life so all our debts are paid. He bled so you don't have to. It's done. Ask for forgiveness, and you will be forgiven...."*

Owen stepped back. First one step then another and another until he hit the wooden railing of the pier, unable to retreat any farther. "Is it really as simple as a circling fist?" Owen mumbled in the darkness, unsure if he could fully believe.

His fist felt like it belonged to someone else. But it didn't. It belonged to him for him to do this simple act—*if* he was really sorry. Was he?

"Yes." His voice cracked.

Owen squeezed his hand with all his strength and brought it to his chest, right over his heart. He ground his hand into his shirt for the first rotation.

"I'm sorry, Lord, for shutting You out, after You bled and died for me. Please forgive my ignorance. Please forgive me." Owen dropped his chin to his chest. "And I'm sorry, Rebecca. I'm sorry I let you down in my carelessness. I'm sorry I have not honored you in your death." He made another sweep around. "I'm sorry I have not been there for Cole." A wave of guilt washed over him as it always did when he thought of Cole.

Owen lifted his eyes to the stars shining above him as he leaned back over the railing. The sea spread out behind him in darkness. Waves crashed against the rocks below him. "Please, Lord. Help me to fix my relationship with my so—"

A familiar bang echoed through the night. The wood railing he leaned against shook as it absorbed the penetrating bullet.

A bullet meant for him?

Before Owen could drop to the ground and pull his gun, the railing behind him splintered and collapsed out, bringing him down along with it.

His hands reached out at open air as his body fell back in what felt like slow motion.

Only, he knew the rocks below would come fast.

The raging waves roared. Or maybe those were his own shouts as his body shifted out over the water with nothing to hold him back.

He was going down.

Owen twisted with all his might to get a solid hold on something…anything.

The broken railing came into view. He made a grab for it. One hand made contact and latched on, while his legs swung down below him. Little by little he tightened his grasp, the wood slicing into his skin. His body swung from the edge, his single hand holding his weight.

Sweat trickled down, burning his eyes. His blood pulsed through his head, blaring in his ears. He tried to concentrate past it to swing his other hand up. His one hand would not hold him for long. Already it had gone numb.

He swung up and the wood creaked and shifted under his weight. At any second it would snap in his hand and send him free-falling, plummeting to the rocks and sea below.

Death was coming. After six years of praying for it, believing it was what he deserved, it was finally here.

"No," he whispered, his breathing erratic. "No, not yet. Cole needs me. Lord, help me! I get it now. Cole needs his father. He needs to know he's loved. I can't die yet! I have years to make up for."

"Owen? Is that you?" a man's voice bellowed from a distance.

"Yes!" Owen called out. "Jerome? It's me! Help me!"

A shadow of a man appeared over him. He

reached his right hand down and covered Owen's. Owen locked on with both of his as he vaguely registered the absence of any rings on Jerome's hand. Where was his ring? Unless this wasn't Jerome.

Owen looked up, but with the lamplight behind him, the man's features remained shadowed. The next second Owen slid up and onto the boardwalk. He landed facedown, his breath coming in heaves.

"Thank you." Owen pushed the words out. The muscles in his arms quivered with fatigue as he struggled to sit up enough to look at the man who'd saved him.

Nothing but an empty boardwalk stretched out before him.

Owen swung around, looking up and down the pier. He was alone. But where did the man go? Who was he?

Owen sat up and faced the broken railing. Or, more accurately, the shot-out railing. Someone had tried to kill him.

Why? Why get rid of him?

The answer came to Owen, plain as day.

Because he was in the way of the true target.

Miriam.

Disregarding his muscles screaming in disobedience, Owen tore through downtown at breakneck speed to reach the clinic. He burst through the glass doors and past the night nurse to Miriam's room.

And collapsed in relief.

She slept so peacefully even with her hand chained to the rail. She was safe.

He meant to keep her that way.

Owen searched his back pocket for the key to the cuffs and got down to the business of freeing her. Hopefully, he'd have the ROR from the judge in the morning and he wouldn't have to cuff her ever again.

Owen dropped the cuffs on the table and took up his post in the hard vinyl chair for the long night of watch ahead of him. After what had happened tonight he would not be leaving her side for anything.

The light pulled Miriam forward. She could see its dancing flickers on the stone walls of the tunnel.

Another step, then another. The light now lit her bound hands up in front of her.

She'd made it. But where was it?

A small stone room filled dark corners. A table with a candle stood in the center. Nothing else was on it.

She skimmed the cavern from one side to the other and caught sight of a sleeping woman tied up in a chair. Her hair shot up on one side, and Miriam thought she needed a brush. But since Miriam didn't have one, she thought maybe she could push it back down like she did her own when it was messy.

She stepped closer. Something dark made a jagged line down the side of the woman's face.

Blood.

The woman was bleeding. Had she fallen down? Miriam took another step.

The woman's eyes flashed wide and wild. She wrenched against her tied hands and her mouth yelled in silence.

At least silent to Miriam. Whatever the woman said, Miriam missed, and she tilted her head with a shrug.

The woman's head turned and shot back with more yelling, like Mother did.

Miriam was in trouble again. And once again she had no idea why. She dropped her chin to her chest like always; then something yanked her forward.

Large, fat-knuckled hands pulled up her wrists, lifting her high. Her feet dangled above the ground, but she couldn't take her eyes off the hands to see how high. Her shoulders tugged from their sockets in searing pain, but still the hands stayed in her focus.

They flashed with gold in the light. Gold and something else.

He dropped her and she hit the rock floor hard, plunging to her knees. Still her eyes stayed locked on the hands. She watched them drift away from her. They curled into the letter C and reached out for the woman.

Miriam's eyes flew open and felt as wide as the woman's in her dream. *Dream. It was only a dream.*

Wasn't it? Why did it feel so real? More real than ever before. Light flicked on in her room, startling her further.

She wasn't in her room. "Where am I?" she signed.

Owen stepped up to her bedside. His sleepy eyes told her he'd been by her side all night. "You're still at the clinic. Are you all right? Bad dream?" He reached for her hand, which she'd absently placed at her neck.

He withdrew it and held it gently before placing it on her abdomen. "I don't think it was a dream." She squeezed her eyes, bringing the images back. The woman with bulging eyes. The man with curled, fat-knuckled hands, flashing with gold. "I think it's a memory."

She told Owen all about her recurring dream as well as the dark tunnel at her grandma's house that led to a cavern. He listened in silence, perched on the side of her bed, occasionally rubbing her forearm to encourage her to continue.

"You're right, Miriam. It's not a dream," he signed. "Both Len and Frank have these passage-ways, and I'm sure Hans had one, too. I figure that's how the drugs made it into your basement. But what I don't understand is why you were in there alone as a child."

She frowned and rushed her hands to answer. "I was caught signing. My mother would put me in dark places for my punishments. At home it was a closet. But at my grandparents' house, she took me into the basement and tied my hands and dropped me into the passageway."

"Dropped you with bound hands?" His eyes darkened and narrowed.

"Yes." She nodded sadly. "It's actually not uncommon for deaf children to be abused. They can't tell on someone and don't understand that it's not normal."

"I suppose, but I still hate that your mother treated you that way."

Miriam had had a lifetime to come to grips with her past. She could give Owen a few moments to do the same. "It's all right now, Owen. I know my mother's problems went deeper than the inconvenience my deafness caused her. When I told you we don't talk anymore, it's really she who won't speak to me. She sent me away to a boarding school when I was ten and cut me out of her life forever. It hurts that I never received acceptance from her, but I found the acceptance I needed in God."

The dark anger in his eyes dissipated, and he shook his head. "You amaze me."

She waved his remark away. "I'm not perfect. I have my days where the anger is so close to the surface that I have to call on Him to lift me out of it. Otherwise it would consume me and I would miss the blessings He has for me. I don't want to miss anything from Him. Not even for vengeance."

"I think I'm beginning to understand." Owen sat on the edge of the bed. "But right now we need to figure out who is taking out their vengeance by framing you for this crime. And I need to know how to get into that passageway."

Miriam nodded and signed, "Yes, priorities first. If I remember right, to get in you have to go through an opening in the floor. You have to move a floorboard to find the handle. When do you think the drugs were put into my home?"

"I would say they were using your home long before you lived there. Perhaps while your grandmother was alive, even."

"It's possible. The door to the room was blocked. And, personally, I had no desire to ever go in there again." She waved her hands emphatically.

"The smugglers didn't know that, though. They couldn't be sure you wouldn't come exploring your new home and happen upon their storage of goods. They probably started leaking a few drugs to get you fired so you would move. There was even a ready buyer."

"Who?"

"Frank Thibodaux. He's made it known he's first in line, and I don't think anyone's going to go up against him."

"Oh, the Thibodaux." She rolled her eyes while

she signed. "They think they have to throw their weight around wherever they go for people to respect them."

"Real troublemakers, are they?"

"With a capital *T*..." Her hands stilled in midair.

"What's wrong?"

"I'm not sure," she signed absently. "It was something I was trying to remember from my dream, but I couldn't zero in on the image. But I think I remember now." She sat straight up with a mixture of excitement and wariness.

"What do you remember?" Owen urged her forward.

"The hand in my dream—no, in my memory—was wearing a gold ring. It had a square black face. As the hand reached for me, something flashed in the light." Miriam squinted as the vision converged. "I can see it now plain as day. It was the letter *T*."

For so many years, she'd fought to drag that image from the recesses of her mind, and now that she had, she couldn't help but grin at her success.

Owen, however, didn't.

"What's wrong? Why does this upset you?" She leaned toward Owen.

"Jerome Thibodaux has a ring that fits your description. And because of that, his house will be my first stop this bright and early morning. I want to know if he was in that tunnel all those years ago.

And if he was, then what would stop him from using it now to store his drugs—or his *pots,* as he says?"

"And maybe he can tell you the woman's name," Miriam offered.

"Us. He will tell *us* the woman's name." Owen checked his cell and found what he'd been waiting for. The judge had got back to him about the ROR. The release on her own recognizance should be faxed and waiting for them at the receptionist's desk. "Great, your release is here for you to sign. Hurry up and get dressed. You're going with me. You need to identify that ring, and I need you…" His face blotched.

Owen sprang to his feet and away from her.

Miriam leaned forward at his sudden change. "What do you need?"

With a pivot, he headed to the door without finishing his thought. At the door, he signed quickly, "Just hurry up," and closed the door behind him.

A heavy awkward silence filled the room. The silence pressed in on her skin from all sides. A silence she could actually feel. Even though she shivered, she got up and shrugged out of her robe to get dressed. Her gaze remained glued on the sealed door, and she wondered what had sent Owen running.

Did it have something to do with the case? Had some imminent danger just become clear to him?

Was it about her safety? Maybe that was why he was taking her with him....

But then, why would he run from her? Why would he turn his back on her and shut her out? And why did it hurt so much?

Miriam accepted the answer to that question, along with the realization it brought. She buttoned the top two buttons of the teal scrubs the nurse had left out for her. She let her hand fall to her aching heart. Her fingers curved into the letter *O,* for Owen.

It seemed he had found a place in her heart...even though she did not have a place in his.

ELEVEN

Owen paced across the empty clinic waiting room, a tacky lighthouse painting hanging on the wall blurred in his crazed mind. Had he really just told Miriam he needed her? Seriously?

What he needed was a swift kick off this island.

He needed to know if and why Jerome Thibodaux was in that tunnel. He needed to know the whereabouts of Nick Danforth, and he needed to know if the Thibodaux family was running this show.

But most important, he needed to fix his relationship with his son.

Those were the things he needed.

Not Miriam.

Owen came to the end of the room and cut a 180-degree turn, only to face the reason for his lapse in good sense.

She stood in her doorway, her hair draped over one shoulder like a waterfall waiting to be played in. Owen fisted his hands at his thighs to keep from reaching for her.

"I don't know what's happening to me." He spoke aloud. At her squinted eyes he realized she was trying to read his lips. He raised his hands and signed, "Everything's changing. Nothing's what it's supposed to be. Including you. Especially you."

Miriam's light pink lips titled up at one side—a dainty smirk that invited his attention. He zeroed in on her mouth and thought how soft and sweet it looked. So tempting. It would be so easy to take her into his arms and forget about his responsibilities. He took a step and halted, giving himself a mental shake. *Focus, Matthews.*

Miriam lifted her hands, and as slowly as the sun rising outside, she signed, "I think I understand. You're letting go of your guilt, so now God can bless you."

"Bless me?" Owen lightly scoffed, but at Miriam's unrelenting nod, he let her idea sink in. "Bless me," he said aloud, understanding. He signed, "I did ask God for forgiveness."

Her face lit up in a bright smile of approval. She stepped forward with her arms outstretched in an invitation to celebrate with a hug.

Owen felt his own face split in a grin, pride swelling over making her happy. He tried to keep that pride at bay, knowing the last time he'd acted on pride, disaster struck.

He met her halfway and took her in his arms for an embrace of gratitude for all she'd done for him. With his son and for his faith. Only, when she stepped away and he didn't want to let her go, he knew this embrace had nothing to do with gratitude.

Miriam brought his hand to her cheek, tilting her head into his palm. Joy filled her eyes with a sheen of happy tears. But when her liquid eyes fell to his lips the celebratory moment shifted to new and dangerous territory.

The temperature in the room shot up a few degrees, and Owen gave a slight shake to his head. He knew he should back away before this went too far. Before he had to repent for hurting another pure heart.

Her eyes remained locked on his lips, while her teeth bit down on her own. She lifted her gaze to capture his.

A question waited in her eyes.

She wanted to kiss him…just as much as he wanted to kiss her.

Red flags of warning waved in his head.

He had a job to do. He had a relationship to fix with his son. He needed to do the right thing this time.

And he would. Right after this one kiss.

Owen threaded his fingers through her long, silky hair, as he'd wanted to when she first walked into the room. Her golden-red strands slipped through his fingers like fine sand on the seashore. He cupped the back of her head to pull her toward him, resting his forehead on hers.

A puff of air wafted from her parted lips. It encouraged him to continue. His own breath picked up speed as the waving red flags blurred away and all that mattered in this moment was Miriam. Here, in his arms.

Owen brushed his lips against hers, promising to keep it tender and sweet.

A little more pressure, and he forgot what he'd promised.

Having her in his arms rocked him to his core. His simple kiss became an astounding crush of awe and amazement. He lifted her from the floor, needing to be even closer to this woman. This woman who changed everything. This woman who showed him how wrong he'd been on so many accounts. This woman who showed him how to hear with his heart.

Except, if he really listened to his heart, then he would hear it telling him to let her go.

God was giving him a second chance to make things right with his son. He had years of pain to fix, and he would not mess up again. He had a broom to pick up, as Len had stated.

But that did not include Miriam. He had a life to pick up with his son.

Owen tore himself away from her. Immediately he ached to hold her again, but he pushed the need aside to make her understand. To make himself understand.

Owen stepped back and signed, "You've helped me so much. And I will be forever grateful, but—"

Miriam stopped him by covering his hands. She shook her head and signed. "Not right now. We can talk later. After everything's been cleared up and the right person is behind bars."

Owen nodded. "Later," he signed, but deep down he knew later he would be gone.

As Owen and Miriam stood in the entrance of the Thibodaux home up on the bluffs, he texted Wes in between his doorbell rings and his door knocker pulls.

The text to Wes read, The Hunter basement has a secret passageway. Trapdoor in the floor. Check it out. Get back to me. I'm about to question the Thibodaux family.

The door cracked open after another round of knocking. "Can I help you?" Alec Thibodaux peeked out, his gaze bouncing from Miriam to Owen and back to Miriam. "Ms. Hunter?" he shouted slowly. "I'm sorry to hear about your arrest! If there's anything my family can do for you, please say the word…or sign." Alec cringed. "I'm sorry, that didn't come out right, but I wasn't expecting you. You've kind of caught me off guard."

Owen would give the guy a break for his crass-ness because it was 6:30 a.m., but by the looks of his pressed yachting clothes and neatly combed hair, it would seem Alec had been up for a while. Expecting somebody even—someone with a lot of money he needed to impress with his expensive digs.

"I see janitor jobs pay a lot these days." Owen dropped his gaze to the spit-shined shoes. "Are those handmade?"

"Excuse me?" The door widened. "They were a gift, and I would appreciate you using the correct term for my employment." He shot a glance at Miriam, who stood plastered to Owen's side.

The shoes could be a gift, Owen figured. Perhaps from his brother? Or was there someone Owen was missing? "May we come in? We need to speak with Jerome," he asked.

"Is this about his son? Is that why you brought the deaf and dumb one?" Alec whispered the last part and jerked his head in Miriam's direction.

Owen knew Miriam read Alec's lips no matter how low he spoke. He hated that she had to bear such ignorance. He expected to find hurt-filled eyes when she looked at him. Instead, her eyes jumped with glee. She winked and flashed Alec her beautiful smile. The older man swallowed hard at the serene vision beaming at him. Owen would say the guy was lost, but with his own throat tightening, he couldn't say much of anything at the moment.

She captured Owen's gaze with a twisted grin and signed, "This janitor has pushed his last broom."

"What did she say?" Alec demanded, his head bouncing like a Ping-Pong ball between them.

"She said, uh, you're a great custodial engineer, and she's happy to have you on her staff." Owen grinned. So this was what it felt like to be on this side of Miriam's humor. He had to admit it was fun. Wes needed to lighten up. Just because Miriam had a sense of humor didn't make her a dishonest criminal.

"Oh, I didn't know you could sign," Alec alerted Owen to the fact he'd just given his secret away.

Owen attempted to skim right past his slipup. "Just a few signs here and there. So is Jerome here?"

"No, sorry. He never returned home last night. Had some matters to take care of, he said, but I'll be sure to tell him you two stopped by."

"Great. I appreciate that. It's important that I talk to him."

"Is Ben that troublesome? That boy needs to learn to do what he's told." Alec's well-pruned composure flared at the edges. "I've told Jerome for years to rein his son in before he started walking on the wrong side of the law."

"I didn't say he was on the wrong side of the law," Owen pointed out.

"That's right." Alec squared him up. "You're just a teacher."

Owen felt Miriam squeeze his arm. She read

Alec's vibe loud and clear. It appeared Alec might know who Owen was. *What* he was.

Miriam's keen awareness surprised him. She seemed to have a good grasp at reading people's emotions and objectives and not just their lips. Contrary to his earlier belief that deaf people couldn't be principals of a hearing school, Owen began to think maybe Miriam could hold her own against the toughest of offenders sent to her office. In fact, she probably had them shaking in their sneakers, wondering how she had the ability to read into their souls.

"If Jerome's not here, then I need to speak with Frank."

"My father's sleeping right now. He's very ill, if you couldn't tell when you met him last night."

"I could tell fine, but I need to ask him a quick question about a ring."

"What ring?"

"The ring Jerome wears. I was wondering where it came from."

"The Thibodaux ring?"

"Yes. The one with the letter *T*."

"Well, that's no big secret. It came from my father and his father before him. It gets passed down from one heir to the next when they turn eighteen. Why?"

"So soon it'll be Ben's?" Owen asked.

Alec shrugged. "I suppose."

"Great, that's all I wanted to know. Thanks for

your help. Be sure to tell Jerome we stopped by. And give my best to your dad." Owen turned to leave. "Oh, one more thing. Do you have a son?"

Alec's chest puffed. "I have two sons and a daughter. You met them last night. My boys sat beside me at the table."

"Oh, right. Sorry I didn't get to meet them formally. They looked like a couple of strong young men. Good for you."

Alec shut the door before another word could be spoken.

Owen led Miriam down the walk to his borrowed deputy's vehicle. He supposed he shouldn't be surprised his cover was blown; driving around in this thing was a dead giveaway. He just hadn't had time to borrow another vehicle or locate the truck.

He also figured the time had come to start showing his badge.

Owen paused before he opened the passenger door for Miriam and signed, "So, what do you think?"

Her lips frowned at the edges. "This reminds me of Esau and Jacob's story in the Bible. When the younger son received from his father the older son's blessing. It would seem Alec's father gave his blessing to the younger son, too."

Owen nodded in contemplation. "That's got to make Alec pretty mad."

Miriam's face turned solemn. "Or hurt. Esau never received the acceptance he needed from his

father. And it was the younger son who used un-
derhanded tricks to steal what rightfully belonged
to the eldest."

Owen chewed on that tidbit for a moment. "More
reason to find Jerome, I'd say." He checked his cell
phone and found no answer from Wes yet.

"Where to next?" Miriam asked.

"Nick Danforth's. Remember when I said you'd
have your day with Nick?"

Miriam nodded.

"Get ready, sweetheart. Your day has arrived."

Miriam brought her hand down on Nick's white
seaside-cabin door. After ten slaps on the hard wood,
her palm stung.

Owen peered through the windowpane beside the
door. "I don't think anyone's home," he signed.

"But Nick's car is here." She gestured to the black
VW Rabbit parked in the narrow, shell-crunched
street behind them.

"It could have been here since before his assault,"
Owen speculated with a bearer-of-bad-news expression. "Maybe he never made it home."

Miriam flattened her palm to bang again in growing desperation. Regardless of what Nick had done
to ruin her reputation with the islanders, she didn't
want anything to happen to him. Someone had already beaten him up to get to her. Whoever wanted
her off this island was willing to go to extremes.

Nick didn't need to pay for her stubbornness at not heeding their warnings.

Owen covered her hand on the door. He brought his finger to his lips to shush her, then signed, "I think I hear something. A jingling sound. It sounds familiar…almost like the sound I heard at the school when I found you in the bathroom." He turned an ear to the door, his eyes downcast, unseeing. "There's a woman inside. She's telling us to hold on."

"A *woman?*" Miriam signed in disbelief. Owen might as well have said Santa Claus. Nick didn't have a woman in his life. He would have told her if he was serious about someone. Owen had to be hearing wrong.

The door swung open to a mussed-up and teary-eyed Stephanie Miller.

Miriam blinked a few times at her secretary before signing, "What are you doing here? And where is Nick?" Thankfully, Owen filled in as interpreter without being asked. Although she was pretty sure he had the same questions she did.

"He…bed. I…here…won't wake up." Even with understanding only a portion of Stephanie's distraught words, Miriam grasped the most important part.

Her friend was hurt.

They rushed past Stephanie and an overturned living/dining room. Out of the corner of her eye Miriam saw a broken chair leg on the carpet. Was all this from the first assault? Or had there been another?

They ran to Nick's bedroom and saw him sprawled out on the bed. Owen jostled him, first on his chest, then his jaw. He ripped open Nick's shirt. Miriam could tell Owen shouted at Nick to wake up. She opened her mouth to speak, deeming it necessary, but before she could form a word, Nick's eyes sliced open. His lips mumbled something unreadable.

Owen faced her, "He's okay. I think he might have taken something, judging by his grogginess."

"Taken something. Like what?" Miriam asked.

Owen scanned the room. "Some kind of drug."

"Nick would never take drugs." Miriam wanted to back her friend wholeheartedly, but with Stephanie standing at the footboard, Miriam questioned if she really knew Nick at all.

She caught sight of Stephanie's coat hanging from the closet door hook. It looked right at home—as though it had hung there many times before.

Miriam tapped Owen's arm to get his attention. "Ask her if she's been here before."

"Yes," Stephanie answered Owen. "We've been seeing each other in private."

Owen started to translate, but Miriam cut him off. "I got it." She signed to Nick, "Is this true?"

She took his refusal to answer as a yes.

Miriam felt the first boiling bubble of her anger

burst. "I know you've been misinterpreting my words, too, Nick. Why? All I want to know is why?"

Nick's stare seared her before he flipped over on his side, giving her his back.

He'd shut her out.

Just like her mother.

Miriam closed her eyes, breathing through the effect from that memory. This was when she normally would have prayed *slow to anger*, but couldn't make herself say it. Right now she wanted to get mad. She wanted give Nick everything he had coming to him. How dare he do the one thing he knew would hurt her?

Tears pricked her eyes. She hated that more. Why was she crying? Miriam covered her face to hide her tears.

Tears…not anger.

Could it be that what she had in her was not anger after all, but a deep sadness? Rooted back to when the little girl in her worked so hard to show her mother she was worth her love? If only she would accept her. If only she would talk to her.

Instead she shut her out.

Just as Nick had. Miriam had to face that this might be her life. That no matter what she did, she would never prove her worth to anyone.

Owen pulled her hands from her face and studied her with his intense onyx irises.

Lord, is this man any different? Miriam prayed

that Owen was different. He had to be. A little boy's life depended on it. Cole needed Owen's unconditional love.

He rubbed away the tears on her cheek. *So gentle,* she thought and breathed more easily. Owen's differences showed in his touch and compassion. Hadn't he demonstrated his acceptance of her when he'd refused to handcuff her right hand? He was different.

He withdrew his hand to sign, "I need to get you out of here. It's not safe."

Miriam noticed her secretary standing by the exit, her arms crossed at her chest. "What's going on?" Miriam signed to Owen.

"Look on the nightstand. There's a gold bracelet. Do you own anything like that?"

Miriam glanced at the wooden surface and saw the piece of jewelry. She shook her head. "I don't wear jewelry around my wrist. It gets in the way of signing. Why?"

Owen eyed Stephanie. Something about that bracelet had him shielding her from her secretary. He took hold of Miriam's hand and pulled her back through the cottage. At the cruiser, they shuffled inside across the driver's seat.

"What's going on?" she asked again with a frustrated hand.

"I saw one of those bracelets on the floor of your car before it went up in flames. I'm thinking it was

Stephanie who locked you in the bathroom and hid your car in the woods."

"Seriously?" Her hands shook at what else this might mean. "Do you think Nick helped her?"

"On the night you were locked in that bathroom, Nick came back. I'm thinking he's working with her."

This was worse than shutting her out. If Nick had locked her in that room, then he really was like her mother.

In a daze, Miriam faced the passenger window. A mother and child rolling a red ball in the yard next door caught her eye.

The little girl looked so happy. Both of them wore huge smiles that told Miriam they were laughing together.

"Once upon a time I would have given anything to laugh with my mother like that. Even my right hand."

Owen didn't respond.

Miriam twisted in her seat to find him sullen, watching the parent and child, too.

She leaned in, having an idea why. "It's not too late for you and your son, Owen." She touched his forearm, doing her best to dredge up a smile to encourage him.

Owen withdrew her hand but didn't push her away. He studied her palm while he traced circles over it with his thumb. He let go to look straight at her and sign, "I'm no better than Nick. No better than your mother. I've been just like them. But I hope you're right. I hope it's not too late for Cole and me."

Owen hesitated. A weird expression crossed his face. Weird, but not unfamiliar.

Miriam remembered that look when lifeguard Andy had ended their relationship. The "I don't want to hurt you, but I'm about to" look.

But this didn't make sense. Owen had kissed her that morning. Her lips still tingled where he had touched her so intimately. She had to be reading his expression wrong now. Maybe he still worried that he wouldn't be able to accept his son.

That had to be it. She lifted her hands to reply, "It's not too late, and I hope that I can help—"

Owen flinched and reached for his cell phone.

A text disrupted them.

Talk about the most ill-timed moment. Nerves quivered in her belly while she waited.

Owen dropped the cell to the seat between them and started the engine.

"Buckle up," he signed.

"Wait." This was important. Miriam needed to finish what was on her heart, but Owen hit Reverse and sped out down the street. "Where are we going?"

"Your house." He shot her a grave look with one hand on the wheel and one in the air to sign. "The drugs are gone."

TWELVE

"What is *she* doing here?" Wes bellowed as soon as Owen and Miriam entered the basement room. "She's in custody." Wes jabbed a finger in Miriam's direction.

Owen replied, "First of all, I told you I would guard her, which I am. Second, she's got an ROR."

"You went above me? I could have your badge for this."

"Oh, forget about it, Wes. You know as well as I do that she's not guilty. Look around you." He referenced the empty room that the marijuana packages had filled yesterday. "This room was locked up from the outside. You put one of your own men out there to guard it. Those drugs went out the same way they came in." Owen pointed a square outline on the floor. "Through the trapdoor."

"That doesn't mean she's not involved." Wes squinted in Miriam's direction. "She could have had her accomplice take it out. That would be a lot of money to lose, I'm thinking."

Miriam tugged Owen's hand. He noticed a masked fear darkening her eyes as she led him to the trap-door.

A conflict of pride and protectiveness warred within him. Her bravery to be there astounded him, but he couldn't shut out the part of him that wanted to tear her from the room and burn the place down so she would never have to revisit it again.

As though she could read his mind, she signed, "I'm okay. I want to do this."

Owen bit down on the backs of his teeth, hating that he had to let her. "Show me how to open it."

They bent down together. She felt around until she found the right board and lifted it to reveal a handle. "Turn it and pull it up."

As he pulled, a sound upstairs alerted him to someone entering the house.

Wes said, "I'll be right back." His lips curled with derision as he pointed his finger at Miriam. "You better not run off."

"Yeah, like she's going to run off in a dark tunnel," Owen retorted. "Where would she go?"

"If she knows how to open this, then it would seem she would know where it leads. She may have fooled the school board into giving her a job, but she hasn't fooled me," Wes replied, tossing his flashlight to Owen.

"Man, what is your problem?" Owen caught the flashlight with one hand.

"Oh, please. You said so yourself—you couldn't believe a deaf person could be the principal of a hearing school." Wes stomped out of the room.

Owen whipped around to find a quizzical expression scrunching Miriam's face. Had she understood?

The trapdoor became his focus. He felt sick knowing she probably had. Owen threw open the hatch in a harsh, quick movement. A black pit loomed below. Cool air rushed at his face as he strained to see the bottom. Remembering Miriam had been dropped into this hole with bound hands had him chancing a glance in her direction again.

Her face blanched. She signed, "You go first. I'll follow."

Willingly she agreed to relive her nightmare. This had to be pure torture for her. "You're not going in alone," he signed. "I'm with you all the way. It's not the same as before. Understand?"

A hint of a shaking smile curved up one corner of her mouth. Owen stood and brought a finger up to stop the quivering. It lingered on her soft, parted lips, which calmed beneath his touch.

But his earlier hurtful words pulled him back. If Miriam knew what he'd said, she would be crushed. He yanked himself away to hide the truth in the darkness below.

His feet clomped down on the wooden steps.

Miriam followed him, brushing up against his back when she hit the bottom. Her breath came shallow and fast on the back of his neck. He should distance himself from her, but in the dark he could forget he'd failed her just as he had failed his son.

He'd failed to see them as people before he saw their deafness.

Owen felt her trembling hands on his back. He understood how she feared the dark—the place where she stopped existing.

Owen faced her to take her in his arms. He pressed her into his chest, wanting her to feel his heartbeat. He wanted to remind her that he would walk right beside her the whole way. His fingers trailed into her long, silky strands and up toward her scalp. The tips of his fingers left lasting sensory impressions to carry her through the passageway.

And for him to carry the memory of her when he left her for good.

Owen flicked on the flashlight. The high-powered beam revealed the sharp angles of dark rock that would surround them for the hopefully brief excursion.

"Better?" he signed after she lifted her head to see the passage. Her hand still gripped the back of his shirt. With one final sweep down her hair, he stepped back out of her grasp. "Tap me if you want to sign, and I'll put the light on you. Okay?"

"Yes," she signed with wide-eyed intensity.

With a flick of his wrist, the beam diverted to the

narrow passage to their right. Before he could take a step, he felt her tap his shoulder. He put her back into the light.

"Thank you, Owen," she signed. Something so simple, but after she spelled out his name, she put the letter *O* over her heart. She gave him his own name sign. Her words to Cole came back. *It's more special when it comes from someone who loves you.*

Loves you.

He shouldn't be surprised she felt this way. Truth be told, her feelings thrilled him. But regardless of that, they had no future, and Owen couldn't let her go on thinking they did. He had a relationship to fix with his son. And she deserved someone who didn't struggle with her deafness. Someone who didn't see it as a disability, but rather a quality that made her unique. "That's not necessary," he signed and turned away.

After about twenty steps, Miriam tapped him again. He bathed her in the light's glow. "Is there a problem with calling you that? I only wanted you to know how important you are to me."

Owen's jaw twitched. "Let's keep things business, okay?"

Shock marred her face. The eerie light beam hid none of her disappointment. "Sure," she signed flippantly. "Let's forget it, Owen." She spelled out his name slowly and clearly. She got his message, and he got hers. He was here for business, and she would keep it that way.

Owen put her back into the darkness and walked on ahead of her. Then he realized he'd walked on too far. He'd left Miriam's side. Now he'd broken his promise to walk beside her. What was wrong with him?

Owen pivoted to go back and apologize. He made the sign with his fisted hand and searched for her in the darkness.

But came up empty.

With a growing urgency, he flicked the flashlight in different directions. His apology on his fisted hand dropped with the plummeting of his stomach. He was too little, too late.

Miriam was gone.

Miriam's feet refused to budge. The beam from Owen's flashlight grew more distant with each step he took from her. She should run to catch up, but his rejection of her and her name sign knocked her steps out of rhythm.

She stood motionless, remembering what Wes had said about Owen not believing a deaf person could be the principal of a hearing school. After Wes had spoken, Miriam had hoped she'd read his lips wrong. She gave Owen the benefit of the doubt, until he'd made it clear he was only here for business. Now she knew her reading had been accurate.

Miriam took her first step.

Backward.

Her pace picked up, separating her from Owen with more than just physical distance. Each step away, each blind and jarring collision with the sharp, black walls, smashed to bits the tender trust she had given him.

She'd been wrong. He was just like everyone else.

Miriam covered her lips with her fingertips, remembering their kiss.

Her fingertips lingered where he'd touched her so sweetly just that morning. She wished partly to wipe it away, partly to seal the memory in for always. *Just what I need,* she scoffed as she approached the stairs. *Another memory to torment me.*

The trapdoor remained open above. Sheriff Grant traipsed through her house somewhere up there. She had no desire to run into him any more than she did Owen. She wasn't ready to put her backbone on and face the world yet. She was tired of proving her worth and—in Sheriff Grant's case—her innocence.

At the foot of the stairs, she glanced in the direction she'd walked in her dreams so many times. The opposite way Owen had gone. She would have told him, but his snub had thrown her.

Miriam stepped off in the direction of her dream and allowed her memory to filter in. Each expected turn proved she'd walked this path before. Each sharp corner flashed a memory of pain she'd suffered in her bumps and falls as a child. So lonely and scared she'd been that night.

But not today. Her broken heart and disappointment curtailed any fear she should have had in the dark, tight quarters. She let her dream guide her. At one point she came to a fork, but she pulled from her memory and stepped forward to her right confidently. The open cavern wouldn't be far. A few more turns and she would be there.

Miriam picked up her speed in anxious excitement. She was so close. Would the full memory finally be revealed to her when she got there? Would she remember who the woman was? Would she see the face that went with the hands and ring? She took the next right and saw a faint flickering light ahead.

Miriam halted, wondering if her mind played tricks on her. Was she dreaming again?

Or was someone in this passageway with her? In the same room she'd been in years before?

A few more steps and Miriam took the turn into the cavern as she had in her dream, her memory. Her gaze shot to where the woman had once sat. The chair remained, but it was empty. The candle on the table still flickered brightly. Miriam scanned the empty cavern, first to her right, then to her left and froze.

The cavern wasn't empty.

Ben Thibodaux stood across the room, leaning against the wall and not at all surprised to see her. The gun he pointed at her confirmed that.

THIRTEEN

"No, she didn't come back into the house. I would have seen her if she did." Wes's enraged voice echoed down to Owen from the top of the tunnel's wooden steps. "See? What did I tell you? She lost you like an experienced criminal. She knew exactly where to go because she'd been down there many times before—carting the drugs!"

Owen peered around, trying to see through the dark tunnel. He noticed a second passageway. If Miriam hadn't gone back upstairs, then she must have gone down this other path.

"You're wrong, Wes. She was down here seventeen years ago and witnessed something horrible. She's walked this route a million times in her dreams since, but that's it."

"What did she see?"

"Well, personally, I think she witnessed a murder but was too young to understand."

"A murder? No one's been murdered on Stepping Stones for as long as I've been alive. No one's gone missing, either. Only a few women who packed their bags and left." Wes finished that last part with loathing in his voice.

"Which one of them left seventeen years ago?"

"That would be Rita Ann." Wes shook his head. "Poor Jerome. The man loved her. He still carries her picture in his wallet to this day even though she walked all over him, and then walked out on him."

"Or that's what he wants everyone to think," Owen shot back.

"What is that supposed to mean?"

"A woman was killed down here, and whoever did it knows Miriam could identify them. The guy she saw wore a black-and-gold ring with a *T* on it. Just like Jerome's."

"So you're saying Jerome killed his own wife? Those are big accusations," Wes bellowed, hiding none of his anger toward Owen.

"Well, it would explain why the pranks against Miriam turned deadly. Why someone would run her down on land and at sea. They didn't just want her to leave so they could use her home to stash their drugs. They wanted her...silenced."

And now she could be headed to the same place the last murder occurred.

"I have to find her." A surge of adrenaline pumped through Owen's veins. "Wes, contact Len to find out where these tunnels exit. I'm going through this way."

Owen darted off through the second passageway. He hadn't gone but ten steps before he heard the trapdoor crash down behind him. He sprang around to find nothing but blackness. No light from upstairs shone down anymore. The door was sealed shut.

Shut by Wes?

Dumfounded, Owen realized if he couldn't find the exit on the other end of this tunnel, then his so-called friend had just buried him alive.

"Why didn't you leave?" Ben's lips moved, but with the dancing shadows from the flickering candle, Miriam wasn't sure if she read him right. Plus the gun in his hand had her focus preoccupied.

He mouthed something about her not following his warnings. She surmised that meant Ben was behind all the pranks. *But why?* Why had this seventeen-year-old boy threatened her?

"And now…have…kill you…Dad…go…jail." Ben's lips pinched in anger.

Miriam backed up. If she read his lips right, Ben meant to really hurt her.

"Go! Move!"

She read those words perfectly.

His gun waving toward the second exit on her left helped, too.

Except, she had no idea where this tunnel led.

At her hesitation, the barrel of the gun met her at eye level, giving her no choice but to move forward. Still, at the dark mouth of the passage, her feet stumbled to a stop.

Miriam pulled air from her belly and pushed out hearing words. "Please…don't…do this, Ben. I can help you."

Ben's gun jammed into her back. He wasn't having it. She could do nothing but follow his directions, and in such tight quarters, the defense lessons she recalled were useless. Whipping around while she squeezed through the tunnel wasn't an option.

Up ahead a crack of light appeared. An outline of a door?

Yes. The exit. But that brought no relief.

Instead, she wanted to run back into the darkness. She had no idea what she would find behind that door. Would someone be waiting for her? Ben couldn't be working alone, she figured. He was only seventeen. He was obviously following someone else's directions.

The gun in her back pushed harder. Message enough to step up and open it.

Miriam pulled the wooden door in. Blinding light had her hands flying to her face for a shield until her eyes dilated to a comfortable exposure.

Ben pushed her out into some sort of sandy cove.

A fishing boat called the *Rita Ann* docked alone, laden with large tan packages.

The drugs.

The multitude of them stunned her. To think all of

that had been in her basement all this time. And if it weren't for Owen, she would be paying the price for it. If nothing else, she had that to thank him for. Too bad, though, she was only a job to him. A way to help the disabled girl.

She forced her mind to think on that and to think on how he'd rejected her—because all she could concentrate on was his safety. Was he still in the dark? Was he lost?

Ben shoved her forward. He seemed to want her to board the boat. Miriam jammed her heels into the thick sand. She couldn't let him bring her to another destination. She dropped to her knees. Ben would have to shoot her or drag her. Deep down she refused to believe he could really hurt anyone.

She angled a look over her shoulder to make him look at her. She needed to convince him that she could help him.

Except something off to his left held his attention. Miriam followed his gaze and saw a man entering the cove. Sunlight hit him at a certain angle and something on him flashed brightly.

A metal belt perhaps?

The man's lips moved, but he was too far away for her to read. His facial expression turned to shock, and he waved his hands above his head. Sand flew as he sped toward them. At the same moment, a police boat zipped into the cove with Sheriff Grant at the wheel and Alec Thibodaux beside him.

Alec jumped out on a rock and headed straight at her, like the other man. At the rate they advanced she thought they would both tackle her.

Miriam cringed and ducked her head when they reached her at the same time. After a few beats, when nothing happened, she opened her eyes to find Alec pinning Ben down behind her.

The unknown man now held the gun.

Miriam looked closely and inhaled sharply.

A black-and-gold ring with the letter *T* glinted at her. It had been the ring that had flashed in the sunlight, not a belt buckle. The ring that belonged to Jerome Thibodaux.

The ring from her dream.

Sheriff Grant spoke to Jerome Thibodaux. The man gave the gun over without hesitation. He also took a wallet from his back pocket and passed it over.

Sheriff Grant withdrew a picture and rammed it in front of her face. Breath left her lungs in a whoosh.

It was the woman from her dreams.

Only, her eyes weren't big and bulging anymore. Miriam had thought no human could ever have eyes that bulged out in such horror. It was something out of a scary movie, where the actors were made up to look inhuman.

Made to look like death.

Seeing the woman's everyday, human face in the photo proved what Miriam had seen that night wasn't normal. What she'd seen that night was this woman in the throes of death.

She closed her eyes to relive the dream. She could see the bulging eyes. She could see the man's hands curling. But what Miriam never put together was that they were curling around the woman's neck.

The man had been choking her. She'd witnessed this woman's murder.

Murdered by the hands that wore the ring.

Miriam fixated on the piece of jewelry. It matched the one from her memory with detailed accuracy. The gold *T* sparkled on the black onyx surface. She visualized it curled around the woman's throat.

"He…killed…her," she said.

Her words triggered Ben to jump over her and attack Jerome. Alec went after Ben. So much commotion, so much sand flying, so much was said she couldn't understand. Miriam locked eyes on Ben's ranting lips. She couldn't be sure of most of it, but one word on Ben's lips stood out.

Mother.

The woman was Ben's mother? Miriam put the pieces together. Jerome had killed his wife. He'd killed Ben's mother.

Sorrow for Ben filled Miriam. The woman from her dream was no longer a figment of Miriam's imagination. She was a real person now. She was a mother with a baby boy. She had a lifetime of memories to make with her son and so much joy ahead of her. Ben's mother had missed out on rolling a ball and laughing with her child like the mother and child Miriam had seen earlier in the day.

And Ben had missed out on that, too.

The tussle between the men continued. Alec managed to pull Ben off his father, and Sheriff Grant dragged Jerome away toward the police boat. He pointed to the *Rita Ann,* and Miriam took that as direction to follow him in the fishing boat.

"Don't worry," Alec mouthed to her. "He won't hurt anyone else."

In a daze, Miriam let herself be ushered up the ramp and onto the boat, glad she'd had the courage to speak up. Now no other lives would be destroyed.

But poor Ben walking behind her would lose his father to a jail sentence for drugs and murder.

She cast a glance over her shoulder to find Ben escaping from Alec's hands. He ran off down the beach. Alec took a few steps to go after him, but pulled up short.

He looked at Miriam and said slowly, "He needs to cool off."

She would have to agree.

The boy had to be so confused and hurt. Miriam wanted to go after him herself, but Ben blamed her for indirectly taking away his father. It was best to let him go for now.

She stood at the boat's railing while Alec navigated out of the cove. As they entered the sea, she caught sight of Ben standing on a tall, flat rock. He faced her and raised his right hand, formed it into a fist and placed it on his chest. One circular sweep around grabbed her attention as she recognized the sign for *I'm sorry.*

Ben had signed to her! No other person on the island had ever tried to speak her language. The fact that it was one of her students made it so much more thrilling.

But why was he sorry? Was he apologizing about the drugs?

Ben had absolutely nothing to be sorry for.

Did he?

FOURTEEN

Owen exploded out of the pitch-dark passageway through a wooden door. Sunlight blinded his eyes, but that didn't stop him from searching up and down the beach for Miriam.

Ben sat on a rock, looking out to sea. Owen trudged through the sand to his side. "Where's Miriam?" he yelled before he reached him.

"How am I supposed to know?" Ben's defiant answer nearly made Owen reach for the kid with his bare hands.

He could feel himself shaking and balled his hands into fists at his side. "You know exactly where she is," he spat out. "And you will tell me."

"No, I won't. Never."

"Benjamin, tell Agent Matthews where Ms. Hunter is," a raspy voice called from behind Owen. "Now."

Len and Frank emerged from the same wooden door Owen had come through.

"How?" Owen asked.

"There's a third tunnel that leads to my home," Frank answered. "I put a camera in there after my son was caught using it to steal from me years ago. We saw you on the video and figured you might need our help."

In the tunnel, Owen had come to a fork and taken the wrong route. He hadn't realized his mistake until a padlocked door blocked his path. So much time had been wasted in retracing his steps back to the fork.

So much time for Miriam to be hurt in.

"Grandpa, you don't understand," Ben whined. "Because of Ms. Hunter, Dad will go to jail. Uncle Alec said getting rid of her was the only way to make sure Dad didn't go."

"Getting rid of her?" Owen choked out. "Where is she?"

Frank held up his yellow-skinned hand. Death was coming fast for the man, but not as fast as for Miriam. "Your dad is not going to jail," Frank said. "He has done nothing wrong. We have suspected Alec and his expensive tastes of being the cause of the drug problem. We just needed proof. Your father wanted to do his own snooping before alerting the authorities, especially when we figured out Alec might be using you to do some of his dirty work."

Ben gulped, looking so much younger than his seventeen years. "He told me I had to help him or Dad would get caught and go to jail. He made it

sound like Dad was smuggling the drugs. But…
but now Ms. Hunter's still going to put him in jail."

"For what?"

"For murder. She said Dad killed my mother."

"Jerome did not kill your mother," Frank replied.

"Actually," Owen intervened, "I believe Miriam
witnessed a man with a black-and-gold ring with a
T on it kill a woman in the passageway seventeen
years ago."

"A ring, you say?" Frank's jowls drooped in sadness. "Before Trudy died, she told us her granddaughter had witnessed something horrifying in that
tunnel the last time she visited. When Ms. Hunter
didn't return to live here after the reading of the
will, we offered her the principal position to entice
her to come. We hoped she would put this to rest
before I died. And now it appears she has. It pains
me to say, though, that Jerome didn't have the ring
yet. I gave him that ring *after* his wife supposedly
left him. I gave it to him after I took it off Alec's finger for being a disgrace to the family name." Frank
looked back at Ben. "Your dad didn't kill anyone.
But it seems my other son did."

Ben faced the ocean, his face bleached of color.
"Uncle Alec used me?"

"Where…is…Miriam?" Owen demanded again,
but he had a sinking feeling he knew.

Ben searched the sea in shaky fear, his unspoken
answer loud and clear.

Owen took off for the pier, spraying sand in his wake. "God, I need a boat," he prayed. "A fast boat."

The fishing boat picked up speed, nearly knocking Miriam off her feet. Steadying herself at the railing, she shot a look over her shoulder to Alec. His sunglasses shielded his eyes from her while he faced dead ahead. His jaw was tense, locked in a clench.

Something felt off.

But perhaps the hazardous stones all around them strained his nerves. Even his hands gripped the steering wheel to the point that his knuckles protruded to sharp white points.

Miriam's gaze fastened on Alec's hands. She couldn't take her eyes off them. They looked as familiar to her as her own hands.

A sick feeling churned in her stomach.

These were the hands from her dream.

Miriam shook her head. They couldn't be, she reasoned. Those hands belonged to Jerome. She had just seen the ring on his hand.

She conjured Jerome's hand in her mind and remembered thick, short fingers.

Not the long, big-knuckled hands she knew so well.

Not like the ones in front of her.

Miriam lifted her face to the owner of them. Alec's tense jaw relaxed into an unnerving smirk. Any doubts of his guilt vanished.

Alec had killed the woman. Not Jerome.

The boat jerked to a stop; the change in speed sent her flying backward to the floor, at eye level with a heavy black…*barbell?* Miriam whisked her concentration back to a more pressing matter.

Escape. She had to get off this boat.

The killer headed in her direction. He was coming for her. His stealthy casualness implied her death was near.

Miriam scurried to the edge of the boat. The water would be her only chance of survival. Her strong legs vaulted her up on the railing behind her. She twisted around to dive, only to be yanked back in.

So close, she thought as Alec flung her to the floor like a rag doll. Pain exploded through her skull. Her head had hit something hard…. Not the floor. The barbell, maybe? Alec loomed over her in bright flashes.

Then everything went black.

Miriam awakened to find her hands bound with knotted ropes. She didn't dare jump overboard now.

From the helm, Alec noticed her awake. His lips moved in a blur. She had to compel her mind to pay attention. Her life depended on understanding the plan he had for her. "You…forever silenced… Made…look like accident. Crash…into…rocks. No one…ever find you. Just like Rita Ann. So sad."

He didn't look at all sad about the prospect of no

one ever finding her body. She was sure he would jump overboard in time. Probably make up an excuse that he didn't see the rock until it was too late. That was his plan for her. To make her disappear.

Just like Ben's mother. Just like Jerome's wife.

Miriam didn't completely understand how Jerome got the ring. There must have been a family falling-out at some point. Something had happened to cause Alec to lose his father's blessing.

Miriam understood Alec's pain of never receiving a parent's affirmation, but she also understood one was still responsible for one's actions. Losing his father's blessing did not give Alec the right to kill Jerome's wife for restitution.

Miriam pulled her hands up to study the knots, but something stopped them. She followed the rope and saw it linked to the barbell. Now she knew why a weight was on board. If she tried to jump overboard, she would sink to her death. If she stayed on board, she would crash to her death.

Either way, Alec was about to kill again.

The boat coasted through the water. She couldn't see the direction they were going from her position on the floor, but she knew they were headed for the rocks. She had seconds to get off this boat.

A quick study of the rope attached to the barbell allowed her to get one of the many knots loose before Alec noticed. The next knot was so secure it wouldn't budge. Aching fingers drilled into the crevices of the rope, fumbling for a weak spot to tear into.

Finally it came free.

With relief, she threaded it through the loop to free her from the weight. A small victory, but not enough to save her—yet. She'd never be able to swim.

Miriam attacked another knot viciously, her head bent. *Come on,* she pushed herself, as she had through her whole life. *You can do this. You can win this. Alec has nothing on your determination.*

Just as the knot loosened, pain blasted the side of Miriam's head. Alec must have noticed her untying his handiwork and rushed her with a swift kick to her temple.

Miriam curled up, trying to embrace her head in her bound hands. She couldn't stay down, but she also couldn't remember how to get back up. *Hands. Use your hands.* She directed her body to move.

On her stomach, she pushed her body up to stand in one movement. Alec kicked out again, but she sidestepped, knocking his leg out from under him.

He reached for her waist to stop his fall, or perhaps he was trying to take her down with him. Miriam swung her tied arms again to block his path. He grabbed hold and secured his feet. She wrenched her hands away and stepped back to the railing.

The water moved by in a blur behind her. They were still moving, with no one at the wheel. *Jump,* she told herself. But she would surely drown if she did.

Alec laughed in her face; he had a condescending air that implied this was playtime for him.

Her chest heaved.

He had yet to break a sweat.

He sobered, eyes narrowed to sharp daggers as he shot out a hand to grip her wrist. His hold tightened to a pain that produced black blotches over her eyes. Alec slipped one solid arm around her waist and clamped her against him securely.

Panic ricocheted through her body, sending her writhing in his arms. Her mouth opened wide, and she made an incomprehensible sound. She was too terrified to focus on perfecting an actual word. She sent her legs kicking repeatedly in every direction.

Finally a foot made contact with his knee. Enough to cause her to slip down his side. But it also reminded her to use her legs. They were the strongest part of her body, used to pushing through strong currents when she swam.

He tipped her back over the side of the moving boat. Her soon-to-be watery grave flew by her. The thought of sinking into its perpetual blackness triggered her fight mode.

She brought her leg around to the back of his knee, jamming her heel into the bend. His knee crumpled. She hit his face with the full strength of her arms. Miriam fell to the floor still in Alec's grasp, but another push allowed her to break away. She scurried back to the bow of the boat, prying at another knot while keeping an eye on him.

Alec laughed again even as he wiped a sleeve across his bloody nose. He got to his feet, sniffing. Amused eyes changed to bored.

Playtime was over.

Another step closer. It was no use. He would reach her long before she'd ever be free of the ropes.

Then his gaze brushed above her head with an expression of confusion. She had no idea what caught his attention behind her and dared not spare a glance to find out. Alec's face drained of color. In the next second, he careened overboard, leaving her behind. Miriam shot to her feet. One glimpse told her what had sent Alec airborne.

One of the huge stones protruded out from the sea in the direct line of the boat.

Miriam hit the port side, hauling herself up and over in one clean arc. The single loose strand of rope flew in front of her while the blasting impact of wood meeting stone cast her forward from behind.

She wasn't sure what had made her jump. Her split-second decision on her method of death surprised her. As the frigid northern waters swallowed her, as her burning lungs sliced her from within, she knew she'd chosen the slow and painful route.

As the light of day pulled away from her, Miriam knew she would die in darkness, forever silenced and separated from the world. *Kick,* she told herself while praying for God to find her. To help her. To not leave her here to die alone. *Kick.* She visualized the motion in hopes it would propel her to move.

Miriam pumped her legs, slowly at first, then fast and hard. Her hands reached for the pinpoint of light above. The light grew brighter with each thrust of her legs. She used every last ounce of strength to reach the sunlit circle. With each kick, its circumference widened. It went from a tiny pinpoint to three feet in diameter.

Encouraged by how close the other side appeared, she pumped her legs harder. Their power propelled her up through the tunnel of darkness, closer to the gleaming light. Air beckoned from beyond the glassy portal.

Miriam's tied hands cut through first. Her mind screamed victory. She would win after all. But then her face failed to breach the surface, skimming frantically below it. Harder kicks proved useless in her attempt to fill her lungs. Without air she would sink back down in a second.

Bright sparkling lights flashed before her. Her mind vaguely registered their meaning.

Loss of oxygen. Pass out. Over.

Miriam could do nothing but accept her failure. *Just one more kick,* she thought in her quiet mind, but her legs went limp. Blackness seeped in and stole her victory away.

FIFTEEN

A massive explosion echoed off the cliffs of Stepping Stones. Out at sea, flames touched the sky and forced Owen to push his borrowed speedboat to the max—forced him to push past his fear.

He jumped waves as though the boat had wings. Each vault into the air sent him soaring above the water, skimming the surface before clearing it again for another takeoff. Up and down it flew, zipping its way out to sea. Out to where Alec had taken Miriam to die.

Flames and smoke led the way. Owen prayed fervently for Miriam's safety. *Please, God, protect her.* He didn't cease until he approached the fiery scene.

He brought the throttle down to an idle where pieces of white wood and debris swayed around him. A burned chair bobbed in the water. He would know this scene anywhere.

All these pieces drifting in the undulating waters were the splintered wreckage of a boat collision.

Owen grabbed the radio speaker while scanning

the water for survivors. "Mayday. Mayday. Mayday." He swallowed hard. "I'm out about a half mile. There's a single rock. It looks like Thibodaux collided with it. It's a mess. I'm going in to look for survivors."

Owen didn't wait for a reply. He dived into the water, twisting in the depths to search in all directions. The murky water didn't allow for clear viewing, and when his lungs burned, he had to come up for air.

The chug of a motor caught his attention. Had help arrived? He circled to confirm, but only saw the boat he'd come in on with a drenched Alec at the helm—directing the bow right at him.

Owen stroked toward the rock. His only recourse was to swim down. Just as he lifted his hands to do so, Owen saw bound hands shoot out of the water over by the rock.

Miriam!

Owen would never get to her before the boat struck him. His only choice was to go deep and pray she would be okay until he could reach her.

He lifted his hands in a streamlined position for a surface dive to rocket his body straight down. The motor of the boat echoed in his ears as it sped over him, its turbulence clouding his view with white water.

Owen swam in the direction he'd seen Miriam's hands. He reached the rock and grabbed its slick sides as he searched under the water. His lungs seized with torturous pain. He needed to surface for air, so he shot up to refill his lungs.

The boat was nowhere in sight, its motor a far cry off in the distance. Owen circled around and around, looking for Miriam. He swam to the exact location she'd broken through before. Drawing in another lungful of air, he shot his body back down.

The water darkened, with no sight of Miriam. He twisted in every direction to find her. His lungs ached, but swimming back up would mean her death.

Something touched his back, and Owen whipped around to see a floating piece of rope sinking downward. Except rope didn't sink…unless something dragged it down. Something like a body.

Owen made a grasp for the rope but came up empty-handed. He would need to swim down farther, and fast. He brought his arms up over his head again and bulleted down for another attempt at the rope. This time he saw the hands attached.

Knowing it was her, Owen kicked it into high gear. Water seeped into his lungs, but he sealed his lips tight to stop any more. He moved forward on no oxygen and felt as if he would explode at any second. The pressure inside his head and chest pulsated to a hypnotic rhythm as though it was lulling him to sleep. He couldn't stay down any longer.

A different kind of pain swept through him. He

could have thought it was the same kind of pain he'd experienced when he lost Rebecca, but that had been a pain of guilt.

The pain he felt now came from losing a piece of himself. As Miriam slipped farther away from him, she took his heart with her. He couldn't deny it in this final moment. He had her heart, and she had his.

Owen had to try one more time. *God help me,* he pleaded inside his garbled mind on the fringe of unconsciousness. Owen might have pushed God's help away before, but he called on it now, knowing he could do nothing without Him.

He kept his gaze on the taunting rope that had managed to escape his previous grasps. With determination to prevail in this third attempt, he swooped in, brushing the tips of his fingers across the frayed edge. His middle and forefinger pinched the rope enough to reach with his other hand to get a stronger grip.

With rope in hand, Owen reversed direction and made a direct line up to break through the water's surface.

A loud sharp inhale echoed through his ears as clean fresh air found its way into his lungs. He yanked Miriam's head above water, wrapping his arm beneath her chin. She lay utterly still and silent. Owen jiggled her jaw to try to get her to wake up. Her body jerked in his arms. He hoped that was a good sign.

He kept her face close to his as he pulled her up and onto the rock. As soon as he had her flat, he cleared her airway and gave her two full breaths. Her body jerked again. He rolled her over to expel the water she'd ingested. From behind, he rubbed her back until the spasms subsided.

Miriam moaned and curled an arm below her stomach. He could see she wanted to curl into a ball, but he couldn't let her.

He turned her over onto her back. "No," he signed in front of her face. "You could be going into shock. I need to keep you flat and get your legs raised. Understand?"

Miriam blinked her glassy eyes.

Owen moved his body down to her side and lifted her feet, using his legs as a prop. He went to town on the ropes, freeing her and rubbing the abrasions her bonds left behind. Their cold stiffness weighed in his hands. Their purpose weighed on his mind.

These hands were not only Miriam's voice. They were her identity.

Owen bent his neck while lifting first her left palm and then her right to his lips. He placed a gentle kiss into the freezing-cold center of each of them. Over the backs of her hands, his gaze steadied on her, wanting her to understand that he loved every aspect of her, even her language.

Even her.

Yes, he loved her.

He let the truth sink in and then shine from his eyes.

Her throat convulsively swallowed a few times while wariness shot from her eyes. She didn't trust him, and he didn't blame her.

A motor off in the distance alerted Owen that help had arrived. He had so much to apologize to her for, but right now her safety was the most important thing.

"Help is coming," he signed, knowing she couldn't tell a boat approached them.

Her face remained guarded, but she lifted her hands to sign, "It was Alec. Alec killed Ben's mother."

"I know. It's all over now. Apparently before she died, your grandmother told Frank and Len she believed you saw something that night that could settle a wrong. Frank brought you back here to see if it was true. I guess before he dies, he wants to tie this loose end up."

Miriam's pale face drained even further. Worry launched Owen into action, and he scooted up beside her. He lifted her head, exploring her face for signs of shock. She'd seemed fine a moment ago. He wasn't sure what had happened.

Miriam pushed on his chest with all her might. "Off!" she yelled, as she had the first day they'd met.

He sprang back. "What's wrong?"

A boat pulled up to the rock. Wes yelled from the

wheel, "We got Alec. He didn't get far. Everything okay here?" His voice trailed off when he noticed the turbulent climate.

Miriam gained her feet and gave the water a longing stare. She looked like she wanted to dive in and swim far away from him, but her shaking legs barely held her up.

"Why are you upset?" Owen asked her.

"I thought I'd earned this job." Her hands smacked with intent. "Now you tell me I was only brought here to tie up loose ends? I was not hired for my skills, but only for my memories?"

Owen's hands fumbled with no answer. But what could he say? He had been no better. He deserved her anger more than anyone. Could she ever forgive him?

"I guess you're right, after all, Owen." She spelled out his name with emphasis. "Deaf people can't be principals for hearing schools. We're just too disabled." Miriam turned her back on him and climbed into Wes's boat.

Owen had his answer.

SIXTEEN

Miriam removed the framed diploma from her office wall. All the initials after her name, each meaning a different credential she'd once felt proud of earning, now seemed to be laughing at her.

In the end, the joke was on her.

She hadn't earned the job of principal as she'd touted on more than one occasion. In fact, she didn't need the diploma at all. She was hired by two old men who'd wanted her memories, not her qualifications.

Miriam slumped down on the edge of her desk. Well, her old desk, anyway. She thought how she'd believed she'd come to a place where her successes had been recognized in the hearing world. She traced the letters on her diploma, thinking of the words of her swim coach. *Get out there, Miriam, and show the world how smart you are.*

Too bad Coach had neglected to tell her nobody cared.

Miriam's office door opened. Nick entered and

signed, "You ready? Sheriff Grant is here to escort us to the Sunday ferry."

"Yes, I'm ready." She dropped her diploma into the filled box beside her and stood, hefting it in her arms.

"Here, let me take it for you. It's the least I can do."

She shoved the box into his arms but only to negate his words. "No. You only misinterpreted me because you knew I was in danger and wanted me to leave the island before I got hurt. You thought it was the best thing to do when I wouldn't notify the authorities and leave myself."

Nick's lips frowned over the box top. He'd already apologized for the umpteenth time, but remorse still reflected in his eyes. She wouldn't let him carry this guilt around for the rest of his life.

"You're forgiven, Nick. You had my best interest in mind. Like a true friend." Miriam shook her head, thinking of all he'd done to protect her. "You even asked Stephanie out after you overheard a conversation between her and Alec you thought was suspicious.

"You suspected they were planning to hurt me for some reason and meant to stop it. You have nothing to feel guilty about. How were you to know it was so they could get rid of both me and Jerome? All I can think is Alec must have promised Stephanie a big portion of his inheritance when she married his son to get her to work with him."

Nick winced at the mention of Alec's big, beefy son, who hadn't taken too kindly to Nick asking Stephanie out.

"I'm sorry they used you to get to me. I'm sorry they hurt you." Miriam dropped her attention to the box, taking a deep breath before continuing. "I'm especially thankful to you for rescuing Owen from the pier the night Alec shot at him." She hoped saying Owen's name didn't crumple her face the way it crumpled her chest.

Nick jutted his chin toward the door. "Someone's knocking," he mouthed over the box.

Miriam headed to open it. Her gaze dropped to meet the face of a little boy she would know anywhere. A boy she'd been talking to nearly every day on her videophone for two weeks.

"Cole!" She used his name sign in a fast and excited crank. She knelt to his level and enfolded him in her arms, practically squeezing the breath out of him. But it was okay, because he squeezed her just as hard. She released him so they could talk. "What are you doing here?"

"I'm here to register for school." He hopped with excitement. His blue eyes shone at her with joy and adoration.

Miriam shied back and hoped she kept her smile in place. "On Stepping Stones Island?"

"Yes. Dad says he's moving back to Maine, and I get to live with him again. We're going to live here."

She probably would have known Owen's plans if she'd spoken to him these past two weeks. Or, more accurately, if she hadn't avoided speaking to him. She'd ignored his constant phone calls and disconnected the doorbell from her lighting system. If he'd rung, she had no idea.

Hurt feelings and anger had kept her holed up in her house, not even able to come out to swim. The one day she'd tried, Owen had pulled up alongside her in his boat. She'd kept right on swimming and pretended he wasn't there. If he said anything, he was wasting his breath. After Owen had pulled away, Miriam raced back to shore, forced to accept her swim season was officially over—along with a future with Owen. She blamed the salty water in her eyes on the ocean and not on the pain he'd caused by turning out to be like everyone else.

For the first time in her life, all Miriam wanted was to disappear from view. Never would she have believed she would actually choose to be hidden away. Perhaps she should have stayed in her mother's closet.

Except she liked people too much. She craved being around them.

Which is why she was so grateful for the use of Owen's videophone. Without it, she would have had no human contact for the two weeks she'd spent packing up her belongings. If she hadn't enjoyed Cole's company so much, she might have made the first ferry off the island last Sunday.

Miriam glanced at the clock on the wall. The one-and-only Sunday ferry would embark in forty-five minutes. To miss it would mean another week of isolation. But what could she say to explain her quick departure to the excited little boy standing in front of her?

"Wow! You're moving here?" Her forced enthusiasm felt strained as the need to get off the island pressed in. The clock grabbed her attention again, and she thought the second hand seemed to pick up to a speed faster than her own hands.

"Yes. Dad has a new job here. He gets a new uniform. It's green. I love green!"

"I know you do." She peered over Cole's shoulder into the empty hall. "Where is your dad? Did he bring you here?"

"Yes. He said he'd wait for me in the cafeteria. He said you didn't want to talk to him. Why don't you want to talk to him? Did he do something bad?"

Miriam swallowed hard, not wanting to tell this child that his father might never accept his deafness. Knowing how it felt to be rejected by her parents had her instead telling Cole, "It's best if I go quietly, but I will always be there for you if you need to talk."

"But where will you go? Your home is here."

"Remember how you told me you were lonely at your grandparents' house?"

"Yes, but now I'm going to have a new home with my dad."

"That's wonderful, but I want to have a home, too. With friends and a job I love. I had hoped Stepping Stones would be it, but it's not."

"I'm here now. I'm your friend." Cole's little hands signed such big and meaningful words before cupping her cheek. Miriam's eyes closed to revel in the acceptance this child freely awarded her. For a brief moment she thought maybe things would get better and she could find the same acceptance from the islanders. But that had been her line of reasoning for almost a year.

She straightened her backbone and faced reality. "I still don't have a job." She pushed to her feet. "I didn't really earn this job, and I don't feel right keeping it."

"Maybe you could get a new job."

She smiled down at her little friend's wide-eyed innocence. "I don't think so, Cole. But I am still your friend."

His little chest rose and fell. "Okay. But will you talk to my dad before you leave? He really wants to talk to you. He's been practicing his sign language."

Miriam studied the clock. Thirty-five minutes and counting. "Yes, I'll come say goodbye, but only for a few minutes." She supposed she could bear a farewell to Owen. Although remembering his words still pricked at her heart.

Cole encircled her hand with his small one. She willed her feet to move, eyeing the approaching cafeteria doors with dread. Miriam prepared herself to enter with a few deep breaths and perfect posture. She pulled the doors and jolted to a stop.

Not one seat was empty. No vacancies could be found on the long benches. Even the tables were being used for seats. Every islander on Stepping Stones had to be here. Miriam found the familiar faces of her students mixed in with the crowd and couldn't believe they'd come to school on a Sunday.

But *why,* was the question on the tips of her fingers.

She searched the faces staring back at her. Up and down the rows, from side to side, then front to back. She froze when she found Owen standing at the back wall.

He knew when she found him. She could tell by the way his dimple popped out. The fact it popped out for her did funny things to her belly that made her nearly forget she had a boat to catch.

"What's going on?" she signed with a little hesitancy.

Owen's lips moved, but he was too far away. She figured he was translating her question when a few people nodded their understanding, which was good, because Nick had stayed behind in her office.

A woman and two men approached her from the front row. The woman pulled shaking hands from her suit coat pockets.

"I'm F-R-A-N." She spelled out the letters with tight uncertain movements, looking at her fingers instead of at Miriam.

Miriam couldn't take her eyes off the woman. "Hi, Fran." Miriam smiled and watched the woman gain confidence to raise her hands again.

"We want you to go." The signs were choppy, but the meaning was clear.

Heat scorched up Miriam's neck. Her gaze darted around the room, unable to land on one person.

Fran's hands waved in a flurry and she squinted across the room at Owen, who was showing her how to say *don't*.

Miriam now knew who was behind this assembly—and the signing.

"We *don't* want you to go," Fran reiterated with a little less choppiness. "You are a wonderful principal." Fran stopped and squeezed her hands together along with her eyes. Obviously, she worked from memory. Miriam wanted to tell her she didn't have to finish this. The sentiment was sweet but not needed.

Fran tapped her forehead, a gesture she probably thought would recall the signs. Miriam could only imagine the signs Owen had practiced with them. Things like, "we want you to stay" or "we're lucky to have you" came to mind. All sweet things that only sugarcoated the awful pill she had to swallow.

Miriam tapped the woman's hand and signed, "I think we should call it a day and end on good terms with bon voyage." She forced a reassuring smile and nodded to Owen to translate.

At first she thought he would refuse, but an interpreter is supposed to be unbiased with no agenda of their own, and she reminded him of this by raising her eyebrows.

His lips moved, and his drawn face told her he might be translating her words, but he didn't like what he had to say.

Fran grabbed Miriam's hands, shaking her head with "Please stay" on her lips. Fran jerked back and signed, "Please stay. We want to be your friend."

Air rushed from Miriam's lungs. After eight months of waiting for someone to say that to her, she hadn't thought it would ever happen. She curled her hands at her sides to stop from embarrassing herself more. How easy it would be to say, "I want to be your friend, too."

Miriam speculated that Owen had put the people up to this. *But why?* she wondered, and looked to Owen for his reason.

Only he was gone. The wall he'd leaned against so cavalierly had been vacated. She hunted for his familiar face in the crowd while dampness nervously seeped from her palms. He wouldn't leave her here alone with the whole town with no way to communicate, would he? After all she'd confided in him about her struggles to find her place—after she'd confided in him about her feelings for him? The name sign she'd given him had demonstrated his place in her heart. Just because she'd taken it back didn't mean it wasn't true. He had to know that. And yet he'd left her there to sink anyway.

But Miriam would not allow that. She would speak if she had to. "Thank you. That is…kind of you…but I think…it's too late."

All heads turned to the windows. Miriam followed their lead and found Owen eclipsed with the sunlight streaming in behind him. He hadn't left her to fail alone as she'd thought. She exhaled in relief as her heart swelled and her hand reached out to him. The tips of her fingers came into her view and she quickly tucked her hand away, stunned to see how her body betrayed her.

"So what's your answer?" he signed from his spot. "Will you stay?"

Miriam shrugged, still not sure staying would be the best choice for all. She knew her deafness made many uncomfortable, and even though Fran was trying to speak for everyone, there were people who didn't feel the same way.

Owen addressed the crowd again, but he was still too far for her to read his lips.

A woman with puffy bleached hair stood up in

the front row. Miriam recognized her as the outspoken gossipy hostess from the Underground Küchen. Her name was Tildy, if she remembered correctly. "Please stay," she signed. "We want to be your friend."

Miriam's throat tightened.

Len Smith stood up behind Tildy and signed the same thing. Frank, who sat beside Len, followed suit. "Please stay. We want to be your friend. We're sorry our selfish actions hurt you."

Then the whole room stood up and everyone began speaking her language. Some people said the same thing; others said more.

A mom with a baby on her hip said she'd been teaching her baby some signs, too, and the baby had been less cranky because of it. One girl inched up to the steps and signed her name was Rachelle Thibodaux. Her eyes dull with sadness, she signed she was sorry for what her dad had done.

Her dad?

It hit Miriam that Rachelle was Alec's daughter.

Miriam touched her hand to assure her there was no animosity between them. She told her the sins of the father were not hers to bear.

Owen translated her words with total agreement.

The pretty young lady asked how to say "thank you," and Miriam brought the tips of her fingers to her mouth, then pulled her hand away for the simple sign of gratitude.

Rachelle mimicked with a smile. Her rich brown eyes sparkled with hope now.

Hope of a friendship between them, maybe?

When the room stilled and people took their seats again, Owen stood in front of her. During the commotion, he'd made his way up the aisle without her noticing. "So what's your answer?" he signed.

"You did all this?" she asked with trembling hands and a heart so full of gratitude and love for this man. She wanted to believe with all her heart that he was different. But he'd already proven he wasn't.

His striking black eyes locked on to her in all seriousness. "They mean every word of it. No one is forcing them. Honest. They want you to stay."

They.

His words should have enticed her to accept immediately, but then she reflected on what he wasn't saying.

What *he* wanted.

Could she stay on an island and face him every day, knowing her heart wanted more than friendship from him? Even when he would never accept her as a complete woman. "Owen, I can't stay. But please tell everyone 'thank you' for all of this." She waved a hand to encompass the thoughtful and caring community she'd wanted so much to be a part of. Saying no hurt to the point she had to bite the inside of her cheek to deflect the pain—or else let the tears fall freely.

"She's still saying no." Owen's lips moved as he spoke aloud to the people behind him. He stepped up on the first step, then the next. "Let's see if this convinces her." He lifted his hands and signed, "I love you, Miriam Hunter."

Miriam felt her mouth drop open with a gasp. She gripped her hands together, speechless.

Owen took the next step up and continued with his signs. "I love your beautiful and squeaky laughter that reminds me of all the joy in this life I've been missing. I love your accepting heart and how you hear better with it than I hear with my ears. I love how you show all the children in your life how special they are, but most especially my son. I will be forever grateful to you for leading me back to my son. You gave me hope, even when I didn't understand." Owen took the final step to stand in front of her. He covered her shaking hands. His fingers felt warm in her frozen ones, and she fought the urge to wrap hers in their warmth.

His thoughtful eyes registered pained remorse. He released her to sign, "I don't deserve you. I've been so wrong, and I hate that I hurt you. You deserve someone who will be your champion. Someone who sees how perfect you are just the way you are. Someone who loves everything about you, including your deafness. Especially your deafness, because it makes you who you are. I'm sorry I didn't see that. I didn't understand." Owen dropped to his knees. "Please forgive me."

Miriam fell back and bumped into Cole. She'd forgotten he'd come in with her. She vaguely regarded his massive gap-toothed smile as he stepped up to her side.

"Owen, get up," she signed quickly as she took in the wide-eyed stares of the crowd over his head. "Of course I forgive you. Now get up."

"I can't yet. I'm not done."

"I said I forgive you. You don't need to do this."

His black eyes shimmered. He lifted both her hands in his and kissed the tips of them. He let go and signed, "Yes, I do. Cole and I have talked, and he says I have to do this or else." Owen winked at his son before continuing. "Miriam Hunter, I want to spend the rest of my life being your champion, if you will have me."

Miriam's breathing halted. "Owen, what are you doing?" she asked with her hands while her eyes roamed the waiting faces all around. She had a pretty good feeling she knew what they were waiting for.

"What does it look like I'm doing?" Owen's eyes twinkled. His lips quirked at the edges. "I love you, Miriam. I will always love you, and I would be so honored if you would give me your hand in marriage."

Cole tugged on her coat and signed, "See? I told you he was practicing. He knows how to say 'I love you' perfectly now."

Miriam laughed nervously. She gripped her shaking hands tightly together.

"So, what's your answer?" Cole asked, as his father had. "Are you going to give my dad your hand?"

Miriam studied her fingers. The idea of giving someone her hands equated to giving him her voice. She would fight to the death to protect her voice, her most valuable possession. She searched Owen's face. Did he understand that? For her to give him her most valuable possession would mean she trusted him to protect her with his life. "My champion?" she signed.

Owen nodded and signed, "Your biggest and best. For always."

Tears sprang to her eyes. She blinked them back as she searched the faces of the whole town. They were there to welcome her in. They were there to be a part of this special moment with her. But most important, they were there because Owen had championed her to them and brought them there for her.

Miriam knew in her heart this was not a dream. It wasn't even a memory. She was home and she was staring at her future. Her champion. She pulled air up from her belly and spoke aloud for this most necessary reason. "I love…you, Owen." She put her hands to his, palms up. "They're yours."

The next moment a ring appeared in his hand and was on her finger so fast she was surprised she was able to finish speaking. He stood and cupped the sides of her face, thumbing the tears freely falling now. He kissed each cheek before finding her lips. His breath filled her, and she understood his sigh because it matched her own. A man's search for the blessing of forgiveness. A woman's search for the blessing to belong.

Miriam's arms reached around him, reveling in the comfort his strength offered her. She felt supported already. When he pulled away, she clung to the back of his shirt, unable to let go. Not even when she looked out into the crowd to see them all fluttering their hands in the air. The deaf person's way of clapping and they were doing it for her. The next moment, they all yelled a word she couldn't depict.

"What are they saying?" she asked Owen.

"They're saying *Feierabend*. It's German, but I have no idea what it means."

Tildy spoke to them from the floor and Owen nodded. His dimple popped out in a growing grin before he translated. "She says there's no actual English word that fits it, but it means the job is done, and now it's time to party."

Miriam clapped her hands, then signed, "I love parties! I'll bring cookies." Through Owen's translating, she addressed the crowd. "This is how you sign *party*." She directed them to swing two letter

P's back and forth like two people dancing, and the crowd all shouted *Feierabend* again while making the sign for party.

She'd officially been included in their camaraderie.

Miriam dropped her head on Owen's shoulder, relishing the feeling she'd longed for her whole life. She didn't think it was possible, but her heart brimmed with even more love and thankfulness for this man than ever before. For the first time, Miriam's feet felt firmly rooted on solid ground. Owen had claimed for her a land of her own.

Cole tugged on her coat again. Miriam lifted her head and smiled down to her little friend and, now, soon-to-be son. He pointed to the clock on the wall, then signed, "You missed the boat."

Miriam crouched to his level and replied with her best principal stink-eye, "Something tells me that was your plan all along, mister." She reached out and tickled his belly.

Cole's mouth opened with total glee. He grabbed at his stomach and threw back his head in a great big belly laugh. Miriam giggled right along with him before she caught the tears rimming Owen's eyes.

She stood with a smile and signed, "Surprised to hear him laugh, are you?"

Owen's expression filled with complete thankfulness and joy. "With you, I have a feeling the rest of my life is going to be full of surprises, and I'm looking forward to every single one of them. I love you, Miriam." Owen left the letter *M* over his heart.

Miriam tried not to cry more and signed, "I love you, Owen." She placed an *O* over her heart and held it there.

Together they leaned in to seal their name signs and their promises of love to each other with a sweet and tender kiss.

* * * * *

Dear Reader,

Thank you for joining me on Stepping Stones Island where the lobster traps are always full and romance awaits even the hardest of hearts. And speaking of hard hearts, I was sure glad to see how Miriam softened Owen's.

I think many can relate to Owen in that we tend to hold on to our past offenses as though they define us. When in reality, God wants to heal and bless us. He has plans to give us a hope and a future. The problem is when we fill our hearts with guilt we leave no room for His blessings.

Now, as for Miriam, I have to admit when she introduced herself to me, I had some misconceptions about how a deaf person views their deafness. Now, I am sure there are exceptions, but for the most part, most deaf people view it not as a disability, but rather a part of their identity. The struggles arise when other people don't see it that way. In Miriam's case, her lack of acceptance left her wounded and feeling alone, but what I loved the most about her was that she didn't let these struggles hold her back. She was one tough cookie and full of surprises.

Thank you for reading *Warning Signs!* I love hearing from readers. Please tell me what you thought. You can visit my website, www.katyleebooks.com, or email me at Katylee@katyleebooks.com. If you don't have internet access, you can write to me c/o Love Inspired Books, 233 Broadway, Suite 1001, New York, NY 10279.

Katy Lee

Questions for Discussion

1. In *Warning Signs,* Owen tried to escape his guilt but returned to a place that was a reminder of his past offenses. Can you think of a time where you have separated yourself from a person you hurt because of the guilt you felt? Did going back to the place or person repair your relationship? How?

2. How would you feel and cope if you were the cause of your child's deafness or other "disability" that changed the course of your child's life?

3. Cole, Owen's son, needed his father, but Owen's guilt kept him from being there for his son. How do you think Cole felt?

4. Miriam had a mother who rejected her because of her deafness. Unfortunately, many deaf children are abused. Can you think of why?

5. Miriam understood Cole's pain and knew if Owen continued to shut his son out, Cole would grow up believing it was because of his deafness. What kind of life might he have if he never felt accepted?

6. Miriam made reference to Esau and Jacob's story in Genesis. Esau wanted his father's bless-

ing, but never received it completely. He cried out, "Bless me, even me also, O my father!" Do you know someone who never received their parent's blessing/acceptance? How has their life been affected?

7. Ephesians 1:5 tells us that God decided in advance to adopt us into his own family by bringing us to Himself through Jesus Christ. This is what He wanted to do, and it gave Him great pleasure. Miriam understood that God wanted to bless her even if her earthly mother didn't. How did it help her in her life?

8. Miriam strove to prove to the world that she was not dumb. She told how Helen Keller's first speaking words to the public were: "I am not dumb now." What are some common misconceptions about deaf people?

9. Owen admitted to his ignorance about what deaf people can and can't do. Can you think of what they were? Did you think some of the same things?

10. What do you think is the theme/premise of *Warning Signs?*

11. What kept Owen from offering acceptance? How detrimental was this to the people in his life? What couldn't he accept for himself?

12. Christ has died for our sins. He has bled so we don't have to. What kinds of things are you holding on to that He died for? They belong to Him now. Can you give them up, so He can bless you?

13. Have you ever considered someone disabled without really knowing what they were able to do? How did you come to the realization?

14. Do you know people who are deaf? Does the language barrier affect your relationship? Have you considered learning sign language to converse with them and bring them into the fold?

15. Discuss the two Bible verses in the beginning of the book, John 10:27 and Isaiah 41:10. How do they relate to the story? How do they relate to your life?

LARGER-PRINT BOOKS!

GET 2 FREE
LARGER-PRINT NOVELS
PLUS 2 FREE
MYSTERY GIFTS

Love Inspired

Larger-print novels are now available...

LILP13R

ReaderService.com

Manage your account online!

- Review your order history
- Manage your payments
- Update your address

*We've designed
the Harlequin® Reader Service
website just for you.*

Enjoy all the features!

- Reader excerpts from any series
- Respond to mailings and
  special monthly offers
- Discover new series available to you
- Browse the Bonus Bucks catalog
- Share your feedback

Visit us at:
ReaderService.com

REQUEST YOUR FREE BOOKS!

2 FREE INSPIRATIONAL NOVELS
PLUS 2
FREE
MYSTERY GIFTS

Love Inspired

YES! Please send me 2 FREE Love Inspired® novels and my 2 FREE mystery gifts (gifts are worth about $10). After receiving them, if I don't wish to receive any more books, I can return the shipping statement marked "cancel." If I don't cancel, I will receive 6 brand-new novels every month and be billed just $4.74 per book in the U.S. or $5.24 per book in Canada. That's a saving of at least 21% off the cover price. It's quite a bargain! Shipping and handling is just 50¢ per book in the U.S. and 75¢ per book in Canada.* I understand that accepting the 2 free books and gifts places me under no obligation to buy anything. I can always return a shipment and cancel at any time. Even if I never buy another book, the two free books and gifts are mine to keep forever.

105/305 IDN F47Y

Name	(PLEASE PRINT)
Address	Apt. #
City	State/Prov.	Zip/Postal Code

Signature (if under 18, a parent or guardian must sign)

Mail to the Harlequin® Reader Service:
IN U.S.A.: P.O. Box 1867, Buffalo, NY 14240-1867
IN CANADA: P.O. Box 609, Fort Erie, Ontario L2A 5X3

Are you a subscriber to Love Inspired books
and want to receive the larger-print edition?
Call 1-800-873-8635 or visit www.ReaderService.com.

* Terms and prices subject to change without notice. Prices do not include applicable taxes. Sales tax applicable in N.Y. Canadian residents will be charged applicable taxes. Offer not valid in Quebec. This offer is limited to one order per household. Not valid for current subscribers to Love Inspired books. All orders subject to credit approval. Credit or debit balances in a customer's account(s) may be offset by any other outstanding balance owed by or to the customer. Please allow 4 to 6 weeks for delivery. Offer available while quantities last.

Your Privacy—The Harlequin® Reader Service is committed to protecting your privacy. Our Privacy Policy is available online at www.ReaderService.com or upon request from the Harlequin Reader Service.

We make a portion of our mailing list available to reputable third parties that offer products we believe may interest you. If you prefer that we not exchange your name with third parties, or if you wish to clarify or modify your communication preferences, please visit us at www.ReaderService.com/consumerchoice or write to us at Harlequin Reader Service Preference Service, P.O. Box 9062, Buffalo, NY 14269. Include your complete name and address.

LI13R